Love Unbound: Charlotte's Journey through Polyamory

Charlotte Rivers

Published by BR, 2023.

LOVE UNBOUND: CHARLOTTE'S JOURNEY THROUGH POLYAMORY

First edition. July 19, 2023.

Copyright © 2023 Charlotte Rivers.

ISBN: 979-8223797425

Written by Charlotte Rivers.

Love Unbound: Charlotte's Journey through Polyamory

Charlotte Rivers

Love Unbound: Charlotte's Journey through Polyamory
Charlotte Rivers

Introduction

In the vast, bustling city of New York, amidst the towering skyscrapers and the vibrant energy that permeates its streets, resides a young woman whose spirit burns brightly with an unconventional approach to love.

Her name is Charlotte Penrith, a twenty-two-year-old student whose journey through life has led her to embrace the complex and beautiful world of polyamory.

Born into a world where societal norms often dictate the boundaries of relationships, Charlotte has always possessed a natural inclination towards breaking free from such constraints. From a young age, she exuded a unique charisma and an unwavering curiosity about the depths of human connection. Her soul seemed to recognize that love transcends gender and embraces the fluidity of attraction.

Charlotte's story begins in the enchanting Hampton region of Long Island, a place that mirrors the duality she experiences within herself. It is a land of opulent mansions and luxurious lifestyles, where tradition and expectations loom large, yet it is also a haven for those seeking respite from the demands of conformity. Nestled within this paradoxical landscape, Charlotte thrived, her spirit unfettered by societal expectations.

As she embarked on her journey into adulthood, attending college in the heart of New York City, Charlotte's openness to love deepened. She found herself irresistibly drawn to both boys and girls, captivated by the unique qualities and energies each gender brought forth. Breaking free from the confines of heteronormativity, she discovered that her heart could encompass an expansive array of connections.

With an insatiable thirst for knowledge and understanding, Charlotte delved into the realm of human relationships. She voraciously consumed books, articles, and documentaries, seeking wisdom from experts who had explored the intricacies of love and intimacy. It was during this exploration that she discovered the concept of polyamory—a philosophy that embraces the potential for multiple, consensual, and loving relationships.

Polyamory became a revelation to Charlotte, resonating deeply within her soul. It provided a framework that aligned with her core beliefs—a belief in the freedom to love and be loved without restrictions, a belief that relationships can be built on trust, honesty, and communication. Charlotte felt an unwavering certainty that her journey would involve exploring the infinite possibilities of love's spectrum.

Navigating the world of polyamory, however, was not without its challenges. Charlotte faced her fair share of misunderstandings and prejudices. Friends and family struggled to comprehend her desire to form connections with multiple partners, fearing that such a lifestyle would lead to chaos and heartbreak. Yet, Charlotte remained steadfast in her conviction, refusing to let others' judgment dim her spirit.

As Charlotte's story unfolds, it intertwines with the stories of those she encounters along her path. We witness the profound connections she forms, the delicate balance she maintains, and the endless complexities that arise when multiple hearts intertwine. Through Charlotte's experiences, we explore the intricacies of jealousy, communication, and the endless capacity of the human heart to love.

In this book, we delve into Charlotte Penrith's world—a world where love knows no bounds, where traditional norms are challenged, and where individuals embrace the freedom to forge their own paths. It is a captivating journey that unveils the transformative power of love and celebrates the diversity of human connection.

Join Charlotte as she fearlessly navigates the terrain of polyamory, defying societal expectations, and embracing the limitless possibilities that love has to offer. Her story will inspire, challenge, and remind us all that within the tapestry of love, every thread holds its own unique beauty.

Chapter 1: Lost in the Sands of Possibility

As the sun dipped below the horizon, casting its golden hues upon the tranquil beach of West Hampton Dunes, a figure emerged from the gentle surf. It was Charlotte Penrith, her blond locks shimmering in the fading light, cascading down her slender shoulders. Her lithe form, kissed by the summer sun, moved with a grace that mirrored the ebb and flow of the ocean waves.

Dressed in a provocative red swimsuit, the fabric clung to her like a second skin, accentuating her curves and hinting at the promise of hidden desires. Charlotte's slender waist curved gently into hips that swayed seductively as she treaded upon the sandy shore. Her bust, of a size considered "normal" by societal standards, held a captivating allure that whispered of untold passions yet to be explored.

As the cool breeze brushed against her sun-kissed skin, Charlotte's cerulean eyes gazed out across the endless expanse of the ocean. In this moment of solitude, her mind drifted, consumed by thoughts of love that transcended boundaries. Her heart yearned for a connection that defied societal norms, one that would allow her to embrace both a boyfriend and a girlfriend simultaneously.

Lost in the allure of her dreams, Charlotte felt a sense of both anticipation and trepidation. The concept of polyamory beckoned to her, like an uncharted territory waiting to be explored. She craved the depth and intimacy that multiple connections could offer, a tapestry of love woven with threads of passion, trust, and understanding.

As the waves gently lapped against the shore, Charlotte pondered the intricate dance of relationships. She envisioned a future where her heart could be shared, where she could love and be loved without compromise. Her thoughts wandered through a landscape of possibilities, where gender ceased to define the boundaries of attraction and love flowed freely.

In the midst of her reverie, a sense of empowerment washed over Charlotte. She recognized that embracing her desires would require courage and vulnerability, but she was determined to follow the path that resonated with her authentic self. The traditional narrative of monogamy no longer held sway over her heart; instead, she yearned for a love story that defied conventions and celebrated the boundless spectrum of human connection.

With the fading light of the sunset, Charlotte gathered her thoughts, a newfound clarity infusing her being. She knew that her journey towards a polyamorous existence would not be without its challenges. Society's gaze, laced with judgment and misunderstanding, would be a constant presence. Yet, armed with self-assurance and an unwavering belief in the transformative power of love, she was ready to forge ahead.

· · · ·

AS CHARLOTTE'S GAZE wandered across the shoreline, it came to rest upon a striking woman, whose magnetic presence captivated her attention. A brunette with an air of sophistication, the woman exuded confidence and an aura of mystery that beckoned Charlotte closer. Her eyes met Charlotte's, momentarily locking in a shared moment of connection before the brunette's gaze shifted away, seemingly uninterested.

A surge of desire coursed through Charlotte's veins, her heart racing with an intensity she had never experienced before. It was as if a magnetic force had pulled her towards this enigmatic woman, drawing her into a realm where age and societal expectations held no sway. The significance of their age difference momentarily struck Charlotte, reminding her of the unspoken societal norms that often shape our desires and expectations.

Though the brunette appeared to be exclusively interested in men, Charlotte couldn't help but entertain the idea that perhaps their connection could transcend the boundaries of gender and age. The realm of possibility expanded before her, and the desire to explore the uncharted territories of her own desires grew stronger.

As Charlotte approached the woman, her steps felt both tentative and resolute. She took a deep breath, summoning the courage to engage in conversation, willing the fear of rejection to subside. She believed in the power of connection, in the potential for hearts to find solace in each other's embrace, regardless of societal preconceptions.

With each step, the distance between them closed, until Charlotte found herself standing beside the alluring brunette. Gathering her composure, she spoke, her voice a blend of nerves and quiet confidence. "Hi, I'm Charlotte. Couldn't help but notice the way the ocean seemed to dance with your energy. It's mesmerizing."

The brunette turned towards Charlotte, a hint of surprise and curiosity playing in her eyes. "I'm Amelia," she replied, her voice melodic and tinged with intrigue. "Thank you for the compliment. The ocean has always held a certain allure for me."

The conversation flowed effortlessly between them, as they shared stories of their lives, dreams, and desires. Amelia, though initially reserved, gradually opened up, revealing a depth of character that mirrored Charlotte's own complexities. Their connection deepened, a shared understanding born from a mutual yearning for love that defied conventions.

However, as their conversation unfolded, Charlotte couldn't help but sense Amelia's hesitancy, her subtle indications of attraction to men alone. It was a bittersweet realization, reminding Charlotte that sometimes desires must remain unrequited. Yet, her heart refused to relinquish the hope that love could conquer the boundaries imposed by society.

The sun dipped lower in the sky, casting long shadows upon the beach. Charlotte and Amelia bid each other farewell, their connection lingering in the air like a wistful melody. Charlotte watched as Amelia walked away, a mixture of desire and longing swirling within her. Though their connection may have been fleeting, the encounter served as a catalyst for Charlotte's journey into polyamory, affirming her desire to explore the complexities of love's spectrum.

As darkness descended upon the beach, Charlotte's mind buzzed with contemplation. She understood that not every connection would come to fruition, and that age and societal expectations could be formidable barriers. Yet, she remained steadfast in her belief that love's true power lay in its ability to transcend boundaries, embracing the unforeseen and defying the limitations imposed by society.

And so, Charlotte continued on her path, embracing the uncertainties and complexities of her desires. As she left the beach behind, she carried within her a newfound determination to navigate the labyrinth of love, guided by the flickering flame of possibility that danced within her heart.

Charlotte's past love life was a tumultuous and painful journey, filled with experiences that left deep imprints on her heart and soul. In her search for connection and understanding, she had encountered two individuals whose presence in her life had shaped her perception of love and the need for polyamory.

Jonathan, a charismatic and attractive partner, had initially drawn Charlotte in with his magnetic charm. However, their relationship soon devolved into a nightmarish ordeal, where his desires took precedence over her well-being. The memories of his abusive behaviour, characterized by rough and demeaning sexual encounters, haunted Charlotte, leaving her scarred and questioning her own worth. It was within the confines of this relationship that she began to recognize the need for alternative approaches to love, ones that celebrated mutual respect and consent.

Nicolas, another chapter in Charlotte's love story, introduced her to a different kind of pain. He was a troubled soul, entangled in the web of addiction and self-destruction. While she believed their connection could transcend the challenges he faced, she soon discovered that Nicolas's drug-induced impotence became a barrier to their physical intimacy. This, coupled with his erratic behaviour and emotional unavailability, left Charlotte feeling a profound sense of frustration and inadequacy. Her heart ached for the deep connections she craved but seemed unable to attain.

Through the wreckage of these relationships, Charlotte began to introspect, seeking answers as to why her love life had been fraught with disappointment and pain. She realized that her yearning for multiple partners stemmed not from a desire to escape commitment, but rather from a fundamental need for diverse forms of love and connection. The confines of monogamy seemed too restrictive, unable to fully meet her emotional, physical, and intellectual desires.

The scars of her past relationships became a catalyst for Charlotte's exploration of polyamory. She yearned for relationships that honoured her boundaries, allowed for open communication, and celebrated the multidimensionality of love. It was through these experiences that she recognized the importance of consent, mutual respect, and the power of healthy and fulfilling connections.

As Charlotte embarked on her journey into polyamory, she carried with her the lessons learned from her past. The wounds she bore served as reminders of the resilience and strength within her, propelling her forward with a newfound determination to navigate the intricacies of love's tapestry.

In her pursuit of a polyamorous lifestyle, Charlotte sought to create a framework that would empower her to form connections built on trust, communication, and the freedom to explore diverse expressions of love. It was a path she chose consciously, understanding that her past experiences had shaped her understanding of what love should not be, and guiding her towards a future where love, respect, and fulfilment could coexist harmoniously.

Charlotte's past may have been marred by disastrous relationships, but it was these experiences that ultimately propelled her towards the transformative realization that polyamory could provide the canvas upon which she could paint a life filled with authentic connections, boundless love, and the freedom to embrace the full spectrum of her desires.

The moon hung high in the night sky as Charlotte made her way back home from the beach, her mind swirling with a newfound sense of clarity and purpose. The day's encounters had awakened a deep understanding within her—a realization that her needs encompassed both the physical and emotional realms, and that her desires transcended the boundaries of gender.

As Charlotte strolled along the path, the gentle breeze rustled the leaves of the trees that lined her way. The beauty of nature surrounded her, offering solace and a moment of respite from the complexities of her thoughts. The scent of the flowers wafted through the air; their delicate petals illuminated by the soft glow of the moon.

Lost in the depths of introspection, Charlotte pondered the significance of her sexual needs. She understood that her desires went beyond the mere act of physical pleasure, delving into the realm of emotional connection and intimacy. She craved a deep, authentic bond that celebrated her multifaceted identity—a connection that would fulfil her both physically and emotionally.

Her footsteps took her past the fields, where the grass swayed gently under the moon's gentle caress. Charlotte found solace in the beauty of the natural world, a reminder that love and desire are as intrinsic to life as the rhythm of the tides and the growth of the trees. It was here, surrounded by nature's majesty, that she embraced her truth: she desired both men and women, acknowledging the rich tapestry of attraction that wove through her heart.

Arriving at her childhood home, Charlotte was greeted by her parents, whose presence brought a sense of familiarity tinged with a hint of boredom. Her father, engrossed in the world of business, often seemed detached from the nuances of personal connection, while her mother, a Spanish teacher, radiated warmth and love but adhered to a more traditional understanding of relationships.

The evening unfolded with a seafood dinner, the clinking of cutlery against plates punctuating the intermittent lulls in conversation. While Charlotte appreciated her parents' efforts, she found herself yearning for a deeper level of engagement—a space where she could share her journey and explore the depths of her desires without fear of judgment or misunderstanding.

As the meal drew to a close, Charlotte excused herself from the table, her mind still swirling with thoughts of love and sex. She retreated to her bedroom, seeking solace within the sanctuary of her thoughts. The room, adorned with memories and mementos from her past, provided a backdrop for introspection and self-discovery.

As she lay upon her bed, bathed in the soft glow of moonlight filtering through her window, Charlotte's mind wandered through the realms of love and desire. She contemplated the intricacies of connection, the delicate balance between physical pleasure and emotional fulfilment. Her heart yearned for a love that could encompass the fullness of her being, a love that defied societal norms and celebrated the unique desires that danced within her soul.

Thoughts of past relationships, both disastrous and transformative, mingled in her mind. She recognized the scars they had left upon her, but also the strength and resilience she had cultivated in their wake. It was within the depths of her past experiences that she had unearthed the courage to embrace her authentic self, to seek out connections that honoured her needs and desires.

As the night wore on, Charlotte's thoughts evolved from contemplation to determination. She resolved to navigate the intricacies of love and sex with intention, to forge a path that honoured her true desires and celebrated the vast possibilities that lay before her.

Her journey into polyamory had begun, and she was ready to embrace the transformative power of love's spectrum.

As sleep beckoned, Charlotte's dreams became a tapestry of passion and connection, a canvas upon which she could explore the boundless realms of love, pleasure, and emotional fulfilment. Her journey was just beginning, and she knew that the road ahead would be filled with challenges and triumphs, heartaches and joys. But armed with self-awareness, a hunger for connection, and a profound belief in the power of love, Charlotte drifted into slumber, her heart brimming with anticipation for what the future held.

Chapter 2: Temptation in the Morning Sun

The sun peeked over the horizon, casting a warm glow upon the world as a new day dawned in Charlotte's life. With the echoes of her introspection lingering in her thoughts, she stepped out into the morning, ready to embrace the possibilities that lay ahead.

As she strolled along the familiar path, her mind still steeped in contemplation, a figure caught her attention. Mark, a man of striking appearance, exuded confidence and magnetism. Tall and captivating, he moved with an air of self-assuredness that was impossible to ignore. Clad in a form-fitting swimsuit, his physique hinted at strength and athleticism, further igniting Charlotte's curiosity.

Mark's charm was undeniable, his flirtatious demeanour impossible to resist. From the moment their eyes met, a spark ignited, a silent acknowledgment of mutual attraction. He approached Charlotte, a mischievous smile playing at the corners of his lips, as if he held a secret that only they shared.

Their conversation began innocently enough, with casual banter about the beach, the weather, and the beauty of the morning. But as the minutes passed, Mark's innuendos about sex and dating grew bolder, his words laced with a magnetic energy that tugged at Charlotte's desires. She couldn't help but be drawn to his confidence, his unabashed approach to matters of the heart and body.

In the midst of their exchange, Charlotte's mind drifted towards thoughts of intimacy, prompted by Mark's overt expressions of desire. She couldn't help but be captivated by the allure of his manliness, allowing her imagination to wander to uncharted territories. As they shared fleeting glances, she found herself wondering about the size of his sex, a testament to her growing attraction and the chemistry that crackled in the air between them.

Yet, amidst the tantalizing magnetism that Mark exuded, Charlotte's instincts reminded her to proceed with caution. She recognized the importance of discernment and the need to establish emotional connections alongside physical desire. While the allure of instant gratification beckoned, she sought something deeper, a connection that celebrated the multidimensionality of her desires and offered a foundation for authentic intimacy.

With this realization, Charlotte subtly shifted the conversation, steering it towards more meaningful topics. She sought to uncover the layers beneath Mark's charming exterior, to gauge his willingness to delve beyond the superficial realm of attraction. In doing so, she aimed to foster a connection that held the potential for both physical and emotional fulfilment.

As the morning unfolded, Charlotte and Mark continued their dance of flirtation and curiosity. They shared laughs and shared stories, slowly unravelling the intricacies of their individual journeys. Their encounter served as a reminder of the delicate balance between passion and emotional connection—a balance that Charlotte was determined to navigate with grace and intention.

• • • •

MARK: SO, CHARLOTTE, I've really enjoyed getting to know you this morning. I hope it's not too forward of me, but I was wondering if you'd like to join me for a date this evening?

Charlotte: pauses, considering the offer Well, Mark, I must admit that I'm intrigued. But I also believe in taking things at a pace that feels right. Can you tell me a bit more about what you have in mind?

Mark: Of course, Charlotte. I completely understand and respect your desire to take things slowly. I was thinking of taking you out on my boat for a quiet evening on the water. We can enjoy the sunset and have a chance to talk without any distractions.

Charlotte: pauses again, weighing the possibilities That sounds lovely, Mark. The idea of being out on the water, surrounded by nature, and having a chance to connect on a deeper level is quite appealing. I appreciate your thoughtfulness in creating an environment that allows for meaningful conversation.

Mark: I'm glad you think so, Charlotte. I genuinely believe that genuine connections are built on meaningful conversations. The serenity of the water can be quite conducive to opening up and sharing our thoughts and desires.

Charlotte: It sounds like a unique and intimate experience, Mark. I must admit, I'm intrigued by the prospect. Let's set a time. How about 7 pm this evening?

Mark: Perfect! 7 pm it is. I'll make sure everything is prepared on the boat for our evening together. Is there anything specific you'd like me to bring or any preferences I should know about?

Charlotte: Thank you, Mark. As for preferences, I have a slight preference for seafood, if that's possible. And if you have any blankets or cosy items for us to snuggle up with as the evening cools down, that would be wonderful.

Mark: Consider it done, Charlotte. Seafood it is, and I'll make sure we have some cosy blankets on board. I can't wait to spend this evening with you, getting to know you better.

Charlotte: Likewise, Mark. I appreciate your understanding and respect for taking things at a pace that feels comfortable for both of us. I'm looking forward to a memorable evening on the water, enjoying each other's company.

Mark: The pleasure is all mine, Charlotte. Until tonight, then. I'll see you at 7 pm at the marina.

Charlotte: Until tonight, Mark. I'll be there.

In their dialogue, Mark's invitation takes Charlotte by surprise, and she hesitates momentarily. However, after discussing the details and sensing Mark's sincerity and respect for her boundaries, she ultimately decides to accept the invitation to go on his boat. The dialogue showcases their mutual understanding and desire to create a meaningful connection in a beautiful setting.

Mark: Charlotte, I'm really sorry, but something urgent has come up. I need to have lunch with an important client of my company.

Charlotte: Oh, I understand, Mark. Work commitments are important. We can always finalize the details later.

Mark: Thank you for being so understanding. I appreciate your flexibility. Here's the address of the harbour where my boat is located. It's called Seaside Marina.

Charlotte: Not a problem, Mark. I'll make note of the address. Seaside Marina, got it.

Mark: Great. I apologize for any inconvenience caused. I really do look forward to our evening together on the boat.

Charlotte: No need to apologize, Mark. Life happens. We'll make the most of our time when we meet. Have a productive lunch meeting, and I hope it goes well.

Mark: Thank you, Charlotte. I appreciate your kind wishes. I hope you have a wonderful day as well.

Charlotte: Take care, Mark. We'll see each other tonight.

Mark: Absolutely. Until tonight, Charlotte.

Charlotte and Mark part ways, understanding that sometimes life's obligations take precedence. They bid each other farewell, with the anticipation of the evening's boat date still lingering in their minds. Both look forward to reconnecting later, eager to create memories and deepen their connection amidst the tranquil waters.

Chapter 3: Unexpected Encounters and Shared Vulnerability

The sun began its descent, casting a warm glow over the tranquil harbour as Charlotte waited, lost in her thoughts. Little did she know that fate had something extraordinary in store for her—an unexpected reunion that would intertwine their paths once again.

As Charlotte sat there, contemplating the evening ahead, a familiar figure caught her eye. It was Amelia, the woman she had encountered on the beach, whose presence had left an indelible mark on her thoughts. There was a certain vulnerability in Amelia's demeanour as she approached, a rawness that tugged at Charlotte's heartstrings.

Amelia took a seat beside Charlotte, her eyes glistening with unshed tears. With trembling hands, she reached out and gently took hold of Charlotte's hand, seeking solace and understanding in their shared connection.

The weight of Amelia's words hung in the air as she described the pain and turmoil she had endured during her divorce. The wounds ran deep, leaving scars that stretched far beyond the surface. Amelia's voice quivered with emotion as she revealed the heart-wrenching truth—her ex-husband, Marco, had forced her to undergo an abortion against her wishes.

Listening intently, Charlotte felt a surge of empathy coursing through her. She understood the depth of Amelia's pain, the shattered trust and loss of confidence in men that had been inflicted upon her. It was a vulnerability that resonated deeply within Charlotte, for she too carried the scars of past relationships.

As Amelia's tears flowed freely, she sought comfort in the gentle caress of Charlotte's arm. In that moment, the boundaries that society often imposed on physical touch faded away, replaced by an unspoken understanding—a silent pact to provide solace and support in each other's time of need.

Without words, Charlotte allowed her presence to become a source of strength for Amelia. She offered a safe space where vulnerability could be expressed without judgment, where shared experiences and mutual understanding could bridge the gap between two wounded souls.

As their connection deepened, Charlotte and Amelia found solace in their shared journeys. They realized that their paths had crossed once again for a reason, as if the universe had conspired to bring them together in this moment of shared vulnerability and healing.

In this unexpected encounter, Charlotte's understanding of love and connection expanded further. She saw the beauty in being there for someone in their darkest moments, offering empathy, compassion, and a safe harbour for their emotions to unfold.

As the sun sank below the horizon, casting hues of orange and pink across the water, Charlotte and Amelia sat there, enveloped in a profound sense of connection. They understood that healing took time, that trust needed to be rebuilt, and that their journeys towards love's spectrum would be unique and deeply personal.

With their hearts entwined in shared vulnerability, Charlotte and Amelia began to forge a bond—a bond that transcended the boundaries of age, gender, and past experiences. Together, they embarked on a journey of healing, growth, and the pursuit of love that honoured their authentic selves.

• • • •

AS THE EVENING UNFOLDED, Amelia found herself captivated by the depth of connection she had forged with Charlotte. Their shared vulnerability had created a bond that resonated deeply within both of them. With a newfound sense of courage and a desire to explore the possibilities, Amelia felt compelled to take the next step—convincing Charlotte to join her for a drink at the famous pub in the village.

Amelia knew that this invitation had to be approached delicately. She recognized that Charlotte had been navigating her own journey of self-discovery and that trust was essential in taking their connection further. With this in mind, Amelia sought to create an atmosphere of comfort and understanding as she broached the topic.

As they sat together, still basking in the intimacy of their shared moment, Amelia gently took Charlotte's hand, her touch a reassurance of their connection. She looked into Charlotte's eyes, seeking permission to express her thoughts openly.

"Charlotte," Amelia began softly, her voice filled with sincerity, "I've been deeply moved by our conversations and the connection we share. It's a rare gift to find someone who truly understands, someone with whom I can be my authentic self. I would be honoured if you would join me for a drink this evening at the renowned pub in our village."

Charlotte, her heart open to the possibilities that lay before her, met Amelia's gaze, her eyes reflecting a mixture of intrigue and vulnerability. She sensed Amelia's sincerity and found solace in the understanding they had cultivated together.

Amelia continued, her voice carrying a blend of hope and vulnerability. "I believe that the pub offers a space where we can continue to explore our connection. It's a place of warmth, laughter, and authenticity—a space where we can delve deeper into our desires, dreams, and the possibilities that love's spectrum holds for us."

Charlotte took a moment to absorb Amelia's words, contemplating the invitation. The prospect of further exploration both excited and unnerved her, but she recognized the importance of stepping outside her comfort zone in order to embrace the transformative power of connection.

"I appreciate your openness and the thought you've put into this, Amelia," Charlotte replied, her voice carrying a mix of gratitude and anticipation. "Our shared vulnerability has created a space where I feel safe and understood. I believe that a drink at the pub would provide an opportunity to continue our dialogue, to delve deeper into the intricacies of our desires and the paths we envision for ourselves."

Amelia's eyes sparkled with joy and gratitude, her heart swelling with the affirmation of Charlotte's acceptance. She squeezed Charlotte's hand gently, the unspoken understanding between them amplifying the power of their connection.

With plans set, Charlotte and Amelia looked forward to their evening at the pub, where the atmosphere buzzed with lively conversations and the clinking of glasses. It was a place where authenticity thrived—a sanctuary for individuals seeking genuine connections and the freedom to explore love's multifaceted nature.

As they made their way to the pub, anticipation hung in the air. Their steps mirrored the cadence of their hearts, as they ventured into the unknown together. With every passing moment, they grew more excited to continue their exploration of desires, dreams, and the infinite possibilities that lay before them.

The pub's door swung open, and the warmth and energy of the establishment enveloped them. They found a cosy corner, a space of solace amidst the buzz of conversations and laughter. As they settled into their seats, a sense of serenity washed over them, a reminder that they were exactly where they were meant to be.

Amidst the clinks of glasses and the symphony of voices, Charlotte and Amelia engaged in a dance of conversation, their words intertwining effortlessly. They explored the depths of their desires, fears, and dreams, revealing in the beauty of vulnerability and shared understanding.

With each passing moment, their connection grew stronger. Laughter echoed through the pub as they discovered shared interests, passions, and philosophies. They revelled in the authenticity of their dialogue, recognizing that this evening was not just about the present, but a stepping stone toward a future where love could flourish in all its forms.

In the midst of their conversations, Charlotte and Amelia found solace in the genuine connection they had cultivated. They marvelled at the synchronicity of their paths, grateful for the opportunity to explore love's spectrum together. As the evening unfolded, it became clear that this date was not just a casual encounter but a significant chapter in their journeys, one that held the potential to shape their futures in ways they had never imagined.

In these moments shared at the pub, Charlotte and Amelia found themselves intoxicated not just by the drinks they savoured but by the profound connection they had discovered. They understood that this evening was just the beginning, a foundation upon which they would build their exploration of love's spectrum.

As the night drew to a close, Charlotte and Amelia embraced the beauty of their connection, knowing that their paths would continue to intertwine. They left the pub, hearts brimming with anticipation for the future, holding hands as they embarked on a shared journey of discovery, intimacy, and the boundless possibilities of love's tapestry.

• • • •

AS THE EVENING AT THE pub unfolded, an unexpected realization swept over Charlotte—she had a date with Mark, and time was slipping away. The weight of her commitment to meet him tugged at her conscience, urging her to find a graceful exit from the lively atmosphere of the pub.

Charlotte's mind raced as she searched for a suitable excuse to depart without causing offense or disruption. In a moment of inspiration, she recalled an errand she had forgotten to attend to earlier in the day—a dress that required alteration for an upcoming event. It was the perfect pretext for her departure, allowing her the time she needed to prepare for her date while maintaining the integrity of her connection with Amelia.

Summoning her courage, Charlotte leaned closer to Amelia, their shoulders almost touching as they shared the intimate space of their conversation. She spoke with a mix of regret and anticipation, her voice laced with sincerity.

"Amelia, I have to apologize, but I just remembered that I have an urgent errand to attend to. You see, I completely forgot about a dress that needs alteration for an event in the near future. It's quite important, and I'm afraid I'll have to excuse myself for a short while."

Amelia's eyes widened with understanding as she absorbed Charlotte's explanation. She recognized the significance of commitments and the importance of honouring them. Though a tinge of disappointment flickered in her eyes, she admired Charlotte's sense of responsibility.

With a genuine smile, Amelia nodded and replied, "Of course, Charlotte. I completely understand. Errands and responsibilities can't be overlooked. Please don't worry about it. Attend to what you need to, and we can reconnect soon."

Relief washed over Charlotte as she felt the weight of Amelia's understanding and support. Their connection remained intact, and she could sense that this unexpected departure was merely a temporary pause in their blossoming relationship.

Feeling the urgency of time, Charlotte quickly retrieved her phone from her bag and handed it to Amelia. "Thank you, Amelia. I'm glad you understand. Before I go, could I have your phone number? I would love to keep in touch and arrange another time to meet."

Amelia's smile widened, and she eagerly exchanged contact information with Charlotte. They both understood that their connection was worth nurturing, and the anticipation of future encounters brought a warmth to their hearts.

As Amelia entered her phone number into Charlotte's device, their fingers brushed gently, the electric current of their connection amplifying in that fleeting touch. It was a silent affirmation of the bond they had forged and a promise of further exploration and shared moments to come.

With the exchange complete, Charlotte's gaze lingered on Amelia, a mixture of gratitude and longing evident in her eyes. "Thank you, Amelia. I truly appreciate your understanding and openness. I look forward to our future conversations and getting to know you even better."

Amelia's voice held a note of sincerity as she replied, "The feeling is mutual, Charlotte. I'm excited to explore the depths of our connection and see where this journey takes us. Take care of yourself, and we'll reconnect soon."

With a final smile, Charlotte bid Amelia farewell, leaving the pub with a renewed sense of purpose. She navigated the lively crowd, her steps filled with determination and anticipation. As she hailed a taxi, she marvelled at the unexpected twists and turns that life presented, grateful for the chance encounter with Amelia and the potential it held.

Arriving at her home, Charlotte wasted no time, fully immersing herself in the task at hand. She meticulously selected a dress for her evening with Mark, the excitement of the upcoming date fuelling her energy. She swiftly arranged for the necessary alterations, making the most of the limited time at her disposal.

As the minutes ticked away, Charlotte transformed her appearance, choosing an outfit that reflected her vibrant personality and made her feel confident and alluring. The final touch of a subtle perfume lingered in the air, a delicate reminder of her intention to make a lasting impression on her date.

With the transformation complete, Charlotte glanced at the clock, noting that she had just enough time to make her way to the harbour and meet Mark. Excitement and nerves intertwined within her, heightening her anticipation for the evening ahead.

She called for a taxi, her heart beating with a mixture of exhilaration and curiosity. The drive to the harbour seemed both fleeting and eternal, the passing scenery a blur of lights and shadows. Thoughts of Amelia mingled with the anticipation of her impending encounter with Mark, creating a symphony of emotions within her.

As the taxi arrived at the harbour, Charlotte's gaze swept across the serene waters, the sight of boats gently swaying in the evening breeze evoking a sense of tranquillity. She stepped out of the vehicle, her heels clicking against the pavement as she made her way towards the docks.

The ambiance of the harbour embraced her, a chorus of lapping waves and distant laughter providing a backdrop to the excitement coursing through her veins. She spotted Mark's boat in the distance, a beacon of possibility and connection. With every step, her heart beat with a blend of nervousness and anticipation, eager to embark on this new chapter of her journey.

As she reached the dock, Charlotte's eyes scanned the area, searching for the figure of Mark. Her gaze settled upon him, standing near the boat, a smile spreading across his face as he noticed her approaching. The connection they had forged earlier in the day held promise, and she was eager to explore where their evening would lead.

Their eyes met, the energy between them palpable, as they prepared to embark on an evening filled with the magic of newfound connections. The sun began its descent, casting hues of gold and orange across the water, reflecting the possibilities that lay ahead.

In this moment, Charlotte felt the synchronicity of her encounters, the way the universe had woven together the threads of her connections. As she stepped onto the boat, her heart brimming with hope and excitement, she knew that the evening held the potential for transformative experiences, deep connections, and a future that celebrated the expansive nature of love.

And so, Charlotte sailed into the sunset, her heart open to the enchantment of the evening, the promise of the unknown, and the beauty of the connections she had forged.

As Charlotte stood in front of her wardrobe, she contemplated her choice of attire for the evening with Mark. With anticipation coursing through her veins, she sought a dress that would accentuate her confidence and express her desire to embrace the allure of the night.

Her eyes scanned the array of garments, seeking the perfect blend of sophistication and sensuality. In that moment, her gaze fell upon a white, sexy dress—its length daringly short, its silhouette hugging her curves in all the right places. It was a dress that exuded elegance while hinting at the simmering passion within her.

With a surge of excitement, Charlotte reached for the dress, feeling the delicate fabric glide through her fingertips. As she slipped into it, she marvelled at how the garment transformed her reflection in the mirror, enhancing her natural beauty and embracing her femininity.

The dress draped softly against her body, its white hue accentuating her radiant complexion. Its design, a tasteful blend of sophistication and allure, showcased her confidence and desire to captivate Mark's attention. She adjusted the straps, ensuring the perfect fit, and took a moment to appreciate the woman staring back at her—a woman who was unafraid to embrace her desires and express herself fully.

With her attire chosen, Charlotte's excitement intensified. She reached for her phone and dialled a taxi, eager to arrive at the harbour in a timely manner. As she awaited its arrival, a blend of nervousness and anticipation danced within her, creating a heady mix of emotions.

The taxi arrived, its headlights illuminating the night. Charlotte stepped into the vehicle, her dress billowing slightly with each movement. She settled into the plush seat, her heart pounding with a mixture of nervousness and excitement.

As the taxi glided through the city streets, Charlotte's gaze turned to the passing scenery—bustling crowds, vibrant lights, and the allure of the night. Her thoughts centred on the connection she hoped to deepen with Mark, her desire to create an unforgettable evening brimming with passion and intimacy.

As the taxi approached the harbour, Charlotte's anticipation reached its peak. She could feel the energy of the night air, carrying with it the promise of new beginnings. The sight of the boats, their masts standing tall against the moonlit sky, evoked a sense of adventure and possibility.

The taxi slowed to a stop, and Charlotte stepped out onto the pavement. The harbour buzzed with activity—the gentle lapping of waves, the clinking of glasses, and the laughter of couples immersed in the magic of the evening. The atmosphere was charged with anticipation, mirroring the emotions coursing through Charlotte's veins.

She adjusted her dress, ensuring it accentuated her every curve, and took a moment to steady herself, her eyes glancing toward Mark's boat. With each step she took towards her destination, her heart quickened, eager to embark on a night that held the potential to ignite a fiery connection between them.

As she neared the boat, Charlotte's gaze locked with Mark's. His eyes widened with appreciation as he took in her alluring appearance, the white dress contrasting against the darkness of the night. The chemistry between them crackled, a magnetic pull drawing them closer together.

A smile played at the corners of Charlotte's lips as she stepped onto the boat, her presence filling the space with a palpable energy. The dress, a symbol of her desire and confidence, seemed to come alive as she moved gracefully, capturing Mark's attention with every subtle sway of her hips.

The stage was set—a night of exploration, passion, and connection awaited them. Charlotte had taken the first step in enticing Mark, her dress serving as a silent invitation to delve into the depths of their desires and embark on a journey where vulnerability and intimacy intertwined.

And so, Charlotte set sail on the boat, her white, sexy dress reflecting the moon's gentle glow. The night held the promise of a seductive dance, a symphony of desire, as she sought to captivate Mark's heart and ignite a flame that would burn brightly in the depths of their shared connection.

A smile played at the corners of Mark's lips as he approached Charlotte. He reached out, his hands gently touching hers, igniting a spark that travelled through their intertwined fingers. In that simple touch, a current of connection surged between them, an undeniable chemistry that intensified the already charged atmosphere.

"You look absolutely stunning, Charlotte," Mark said, his voice laced with admiration. "That dress suits you perfectly. I'm truly fortunate to have the pleasure of your company tonight."

Charlotte's heart fluttered at his words, a mixture of flattery and excitement swirling within her. The feeling of Mark's touch lingered, their hands still intertwined, a tangible symbol of the connection that blossomed between them.

"Thank you, Mark," she replied, her voice tinged with a hint of bashfulness. "You look rather dashing yourself. I must say, the ambiance of the harbour and your boat make for a truly enchanting setting."

Mark's gaze intensified, his eyes locked with Charlotte's, as if they held a secret language all their own. The air between them crackled with anticipation, the energy of their connection almost palpable.

"I couldn't agree more, Charlotte," Mark responded, his voice filled with a mixture of charm and sincerity. "The stars above, the gentle sway of the boat, and your captivating presence—it's as if the universe conspired to create this perfect moment."

As they spoke, their proximity increased, the space between them diminishing. Charlotte felt a magnetic pull towards Mark, a desire to explore the depths of their connection and surrender to the intoxicating allure of the evening.

In the harbour's embrace, they found themselves dancing on the precipice of something profound—a collision of desires, hearts, and souls. The boat, surrounded by the serenity of the water, became their sanctuary—a vessel that would carry them on a voyage of passion and exploration.

As they stepped onto the boat together, the world around them seemed to fade into the background, their focus fixed solely on each other. They settled into a cosy spot, the atmosphere charged with anticipation, their bodies mere inches apart.

The night sky stretched above them, a blanket of twinkling stars that bore witness to the burgeoning connection between Charlotte and Mark. With each passing moment, their flirtation grew bolder, their words laced with an intoxicating blend of charm and desire.

Mark's fingertips grazed Charlotte's skin, leaving a trail of fire in their wake. She shivered at the touch, her senses heightened, attuned to every nuance of his caress. It was a dance of seduction, a delicate interplay between two souls craving connection.

Their conversation danced between playful banter and heartfelt confessions, as they delved into the depths of their desires and dreams. In the glow of the moonlight, they shared stories of past loves and lessons learned, forging a bond rooted in vulnerability and authenticity.

As the night wore on, the energy between them intensified, their bodies drawn together as if by an irresistible force. They spoke in hushed tones, their words carrying the weight of unspoken promises and shared longing.

In this moment, Charlotte knew that the evening held the potential to transcend the boundaries of a simple date. The chemistry between them was undeniable, a magnetic pull that defied logic and ignited the embers of passion within her.

As Mark's hand gently traced the outline of Charlotte's jawline, she leaned into his touch, savouring the tenderness and intimacy of the moment. The world around them faded into insignificance, as they surrendered to the intoxicating dance of desire.

And so, in the harbour's embrace, Charlotte and Mark found themselves entangled in a web of seduction, their hearts beating in sync with the rhythm of their connection. Their evening together had just begun, and the possibilities that lay before them seemed boundless—a symphony of passion, exploration, and a love that honoured the depths of their desires.

As the evening unfolded, Charlotte and Mark found themselves immersed in a captivating dinner on the boat. The tantalizing aroma of seafood wafted through the air, mingling with the gentle sea breeze, creating a culinary symphony that delighted their senses.

The table was adorned with an exquisite spread—a platter of freshly shucked oysters, succulent lobster tails glistening in the candlelight, and a variety of delectable seafood delicacies. Each dish was meticulously prepared, a testament to the culinary expertise behind the meal.

The clinking of glasses resonated throughout the boat as Mark poured a glass of the finest white wine. The liquid sparkled like liquid gold, casting an ethereal glow on the crystal-clear vessel. The wine breathed life into the moment, its delicate bouquet promising an exquisite pairing with the flavours of the sea.

Charlotte's eyes lit up with anticipation as she raised her glass, toasting to the enchanting evening they were about to embark on. The wine caressed her palate, its vibrant notes dancing across her taste buds, complementing the seafood feast before them. It was a symphony of flavours, a celebration of the senses that heightened the connection between them.

They revealed in each bite, savouring the delicacies that adorned their plates. The oysters, plump and briny, awakened their palates with a burst of freshness. The lobster, succulent and tender, melted in their mouths, a decadent indulgence that spoke of luxury and abundance.

Between bites, their conversation flowed effortlessly, their words mingling with the clinking of cutlery and the soft lapping of the water against the boat. They delved deeper into their passions, their dreams, and their shared sense of adventure, as if each morsel of food served as a catalyst for connection.

As the evening wore on, the ambiance shifted from anticipation to a comfortable intimacy. Laughter filled the air, punctuating moments of shared anecdotes and playful banter. They discovered shared interests and quirks, each revelation deepening their connection and understanding of one another.

Charlotte's eyes sparkled with delight as she looked across the table at Mark, her heart filled with gratitude for this exquisite moment. She relished in the flavours, the textures, and the company that surrounded her, basking in the warmth of the evening and the promise of a budding romance.

The wine continued to flow, each sip enhancing the flavours of the meal and kindling a sense of joy within Charlotte. The crispness of the wine mirrored the vibrancy of the conversation, creating a harmonious symphony of sensations that swept her away.

As the dinner drew to a close, and the plates were cleared, a sense of contentment settled over them. They lingered at the table, their gazes locked, their connection deepening with every passing moment. It was as if time had stood still, allowing them to savour the magic of the evening and relish in the profound connection they had forged.

In that moment, Charlotte realized that it wasn't just the delectable food and the exquisite wine that had made the evening memorable—it was the shared experience, the laughter, and the vulnerability that had woven itself into the fabric of their connection.

As they sat there, bathed in the soft glow of the moon and the flickering candlelight, Charlotte allowed herself to fully immerse in the moment. She soaked up the beauty of the sea surrounding them, the gentle sway of the boat, and the warmth of Mark's presence by her side. In this serene ambiance, Charlotte found herself truly present, relishing the taste of the seafood, the delicate notes of the wine, and the intoxicating company of the man who sat before her. She couldn't help but smile, grateful for the extraordinary evening and the promise it held for the future.

With every sip of wine and every bite of food, Charlotte savoured the magic of the moment, cherishing the connection she had formed with Mark. It was a dinner that would forever be etched in her memory—a celebration of love, desire, and the exquisite pleasures that life had to offer.

• • • •

TWO HOURS HAD PASSED since Charlotte bid farewell to Mark, their evening together on the boat drawing to a close. The experience had been nothing short of enchanting, and as she made her way back onto land, her heart was filled with a mixture of gratitude, exhilaration, and desire.

Mark, however, felt a surge of emotion as he watched Charlotte depart. He couldn't deny the strong connection they had formed throughout the evening, a connection that transcended mere conversation and had ignited a spark of passion within him. The memory of her beauty, her laughter, and the depth of their conversations lingered in his mind, urging him to take a leap of faith.

Driven by his emotions, Mark found himself unable to resist the longing in his heart. He stepped forward, closing the distance between them, and as Charlotte turned to face him, he mustered the courage to express his feelings.

With a tender gaze, Mark reached out and gently cupped Charlotte's face in his hands. The air crackled with anticipation as he leaned in, his lips brushing against hers in a delicate yet powerful kiss. It was a gesture fuelled by genuine emotion, a testament to the connection they had shared throughout the evening.

For a fleeting moment, Charlotte's senses were overwhelmed—the taste of Mark's lips, the scent of the sea lingering on his skin, and the electric current that surged through her body. In that instant, desire mingled with the weight of the decision she knew lay before her.

As their lips parted, their eyes met, and a world of unspoken thoughts and possibilities seemed to pass between them. Charlotte, while exhilarated by the intensity of their kiss, understood the significance of the moment. She craved connection, both emotional and physical, but she also wanted to honour the depth of her exploration of love's spectrum.

A mix of emotions danced within her—excitement, uncertainty, and the need for introspection. She knew that making a decision in the heat of the moment could potentially limit the possibilities that lay before her. She wanted to embrace the freedom to explore different love options, to truly understand her desires and the intricate web of connections she could weave.

With a smile that spoke volumes, Charlotte gently withdrew from Mark's touch. She looked into his eyes, her voice filled with gratitude and genuine appreciation for their evening together.

"Thank you, Mark," she whispered, her words carrying a mixture of happiness and contemplation. "Tonight, has been absolutely wonderful, and I cherish the connection we've shared. But I believe it's important for me to take some time to reflect on all the love options that have presented themselves tonight."

Mark, though taken aback by Charlotte's response, admired her honesty and the depth of her self-awareness. He nodded understandingly, his eyes filled with a mix of admiration and anticipation.

"I respect your desire to explore all your options, Charlotte," he replied, his voice filled with warmth. "Please know that the connection we've forged tonight has been truly special, and I hope that whatever path you choose, it brings you happiness and fulfilment."

Charlotte smiled appreciatively, her heart swelling with a sense of liberation and empowerment. She understood that taking the time to explore her desires and contemplate the various love options available to her would lead her to a more authentic and fulfilling path.

With a final farewell and a lingering gaze, Charlotte turned and began her journey of self-reflection, knowing that the connection with Mark would remain a cherished memory and that the possibilities that awaited her were as boundless as the ocean itself.

As she walked away, Charlotte carried with her the weight of the decision that awaited, recognizing that she had the power to shape her own love story—one that embraced both the depths of emotional connection and the exploration of physical desire. In the days to come, she would delve further into her own desires, finding solace and clarity in the reflection and contemplation that awaited her.

And so, Charlotte embarked on a personal journey of self-discovery, allowing her heart and mind to wander through the vast landscape of love's spectrum, eager to uncover the truths that would guide her towards a future that honoured her desires, her authenticity, and her pursuit of deep and meaningful connections.

As Charlotte's words echoed in the air, Mark found himself processing the depth and implications of her desire to explore all her love options. His mind raced with questions and uncertainty, unsure of what exactly she meant and what it might entail for their budding connection.

Confusion and a tinge of insecurity mingled within Mark's thoughts. Was there someone else vying for Charlotte's affection? Did she have reservations about pursuing a more committed relationship? The unknowns weighed heavily on his heart, tugging at his sense of vulnerability.

Mark had opened himself up to the possibility of a deep connection with Charlotte, allowing himself to be drawn to her warmth, her wit, and her undeniable beauty. The thought of potential competition for her affections left him feeling uncertain and filled with a mix of emotions—curiosity, anxiety, and a longing for clarity.

He yearned to understand Charlotte's intentions and desires, yet he also recognized the importance of respecting her need for exploration and introspection. It was a delicate balance, one that required patience and open communication.

In this moment of uncertainty, Mark made a conscious decision to approach the situation with empathy and understanding. Rather than jumping to conclusions or allowing jealousy to consume him, he chose to honour the connection they had shared and give Charlotte the space she needed to navigate her own journey of self-discovery.

He understood that love was complex and multifaceted, and each individual's path towards finding fulfilment looked different. While his heart felt a tinge of disappointment and uncertainty, he knew that embracing the unknown and supporting Charlotte in her exploration would lead to greater authenticity and ultimately a stronger connection if their paths converged once more.

As Mark reflected on their evening together, he reminded himself of the undeniable connection they had shared—the conversations, the laughter, and the tangible chemistry that had pulsed between them. It was a foundation that couldn't be easily dismissed, and he held onto the hope that their connection would transcend the uncertainties of the present.

Mark resolved to communicate openly with Charlotte, seeking clarity and understanding while also giving her the space she needed. He recognized that the situation required patience and trust, and he was willing to navigate the unknown to see where their connection would lead.

In the days to come, Mark would reach out to Charlotte, expressing his appreciation for their time together and his willingness to support her in her exploration of love's spectrum. He would strive to maintain a sense of openness and understanding, keeping their lines of communication alive in order to navigate the intricacies of their connection.

While uncertainty lingered, Mark's resolve remained firm—he would be there for Charlotte, offering support, understanding, and an unwavering belief in the power of their connection. Together, they would navigate the complex tapestry of love, each pursuing their own truths while keeping the possibility of a shared future alive.

And so, Mark braced himself for the journey ahead, ready to face the challenges and uncertainties with grace and compassion. He would let go of his own expectations, embracing the beauty of the unknown and trusting that love's intricate dance would guide them towards a deeper understanding of themselves and each other.

• • • •

AS CHARLOTTE SAT IN the taxi, her thoughts and emotions swirled within her. The evening with Mark had been filled with intensity and excitement, but her mind was also drawn back to the encounter with Amelia at the pub. The memory of their conversation, the tears in Amelia's eyes, and the unspoken connection between them lingered in her mind.

As the taxi cruised through the streets, an unexpected sight caught Charlotte's attention—the pub where she had shared a drink with Amelia. It stood there, a beacon of memories and possibilities, beckoning her to revisit the connections she had formed earlier in the evening.

A surge of curiosity and a desire for closure washed over Charlotte. She couldn't ignore the strong connection she had felt with Amelia, the depth of emotion they had shared in that brief encounter. It was as if fate had intertwined their paths, leaving Charlotte with unanswered questions and an unexplored potential.

With a mix of nervousness and excitement, Charlotte mustered the courage to ask the taxi driver to make a detour. She needed to follow the pull of her intuition, to seek resolution and perhaps a deeper understanding of the connection that had stirred within her.

As the taxi pulled up in front of the pub, Charlotte's heart skipped a beat. She paid the driver and stepped out onto the sidewalk; her eyes fixed on the entrance. The familiar sounds of laughter and music spilled out into the night, enveloping her in a warm embrace.

Taking a deep breath, Charlotte pushed open the door and stepped inside. The atmosphere was alive with energy, the air thick with the scent of conversations and shared moments. She scanned the room, searching for a glimpse of Amelia, hoping to continue their interrupted connection.

And then, her eyes met Amelia's across the room. Time seemed to stand still as they locked gazes, an unspoken understanding passing between them. In that moment, Charlotte felt a surge of recognition and possibility—a call to explore the connection they had briefly touched upon earlier in the evening.

With a mixture of trepidation and determination, Charlotte made her way towards Amelia. The room seemed to fade into the background as their eyes locked, the electricity between them palpable. The pub became a sacred space, a container for their burgeoning connection.

Amelia smiled, a mixture of surprise and delight crossing her face. It was a silent invitation, an acknowledgment that they were meant to cross paths once more. Charlotte felt a warmth spread through her as she closed the distance between them, the weight of the evening's encounters propelling her forward.

Their conversation flowed effortlessly, as if they had known each other for a lifetime. They delved deeper into their experiences, their desires, and the complexities of love. It was a meeting of minds and souls, a dance of vulnerability and understanding.

As the night unfolded, Charlotte and Amelia discovered a shared language—a connection that defied conventional boundaries and expectations. They recognized the beauty in their unique experiences, their desires that transcended traditional norms, and the need to honour their own authentic paths.

In the depths of the pub, amidst the buzz of conversations and clinking glasses, Charlotte and Amelia found solace in each other's presence. They recognized the power of their connection and the potential it held for exploration, growth, and mutual support.

With every passing moment, Charlotte felt her understanding of love's spectrum expand. The complexities and possibilities stretched before her like a canvas waiting to be painted with vibrant colours. And in that realization, she found a newfound freedom—a liberation from societal norms and the permission to embrace her desires without compromise.

As the night wore on, Charlotte and Amelia laughed, shared stories, and opened their hearts to each other. They acknowledged that their connection was unique, and they revealed in the understanding and acceptance that flowed between them.

In that pub, Charlotte discovered a world of possibilities—a tapestry of connections, desires, and love options that extended far beyond her previous perceptions. And as she and Amelia continued their conversation, she couldn't help but feel a sense of gratitude—for the evening that had brought them together, for the chance to explore love in all its intricacies, and for the newfound understanding that she had the power to shape her own love story, one that honoured her desires and embraced the richness of human connection.

And so, amidst the hubbub of the pub, Charlotte and Amelia forged a connection that transcended the boundaries of convention. They embarked on a journey together, exploring the depths of their desires and the infinite possibilities that lay before them. In that moment, the pub became a haven, a space where their authentic selves could thrive, and love's vast spectrum could be celebrated.

Chapter 4 Unveiling the Uncharted: A Night of Intimacy with Amelia

A melia leaned in closer, her voice laced with a subtle invitation as she spoke to Charlotte amidst the buzz of the pub.

Amelia: "Charlotte, the night feels alive with possibilities, and I can't help but feel a strong connection between us. Would you like to continue this adventure? I have an apartment just around the corner, a cosy space where we can retreat and explore the depths of our desires."

Charlotte's eyes widened slightly, caught off guard by Amelia's proposition. She hesitated for a moment, her mind racing with anticipation and curiosity.

Charlotte: "Amelia, I... I feel it too. This connection between us is undeniable, and the thought of continuing our evening together excites me. Lead the way."

A playful smile tugged at the corners of Amelia's lips as she rose from her seat, extending her hand towards Charlotte.

Amelia: "Come with me, Charlotte. Let's escape the noise and immerse ourselves in a space that reflects the beauty of our connection."

Charlotte's heart fluttered as she placed her hand in Amelia's, ready to embark on this uncharted territory. They made their way through the crowd, anticipation building with each step towards the unknown.

As they walked out into the cool night air, Amelia guided Charlotte through the streets, their laughter and shared excitement punctuating the silence between them.

Charlotte: "Amelia, I must admit, I'm curious about your apartment. What's it like? How would you describe it?"

Amelia's eyes sparkled mischievously as she turned to Charlotte, her voice filled with a hint of playfulness.

Amelia: "Oh, my dear Charlotte, my apartment is a girly haven, a space where feminine charm and comfort intertwine. Soft hues of pink adorn the walls, creating an ambiance of warmth and tranquillity. It's a place where desires can be explored, passions can ignite, and connections can deepen."

Charlotte's curiosity deepened, her imagination conjuring images of a cosy and inviting space.

Charlotte: "That sounds enchanting, Amelia. I'm eager to experience the beauty and comfort of your girly haven. I'm sure it reflects the vibrancy of your personality."

Amelia's smile widened, her steps quickening as they approached the apartment building.

Amelia: "I'm thrilled that you're intrigued, Charlotte. It's a space that I've curated with love, filled with delicate touches and an ambiance that encourages vulnerability and exploration. I believe you'll find it both captivating and inviting."

As they reached the entrance of the apartment building, Amelia turned to Charlotte, her eyes filled with anticipation.

Amelia: "We're here, Charlotte. Are you ready to step into this world of possibilities? To embrace the unknown and let our connection guide us?"

Charlotte took a deep breath, feeling a surge of excitement and anticipation coursing through her veins.

Charlotte: "Yes, Amelia. I'm ready. Let's dive into this adventure together and discover the depths of our desires within the confines of your enchanting girly haven."

With that, they stepped into the building, their hands intertwined, their hearts aligned in a shared journey of exploration and connection.

As Amelia extended her invitation, Charlotte's heart raced with anticipation. She eagerly followed Amelia to her apartment, located just steps away from the lively pub. The moment the door swung open, Charlotte found herself immersed in a world that exuded femininity and charm.

The apartment was a reflection of Amelia's personality—vibrant, stylish, and unapologetically feminine. Soft hues of pink adorned the walls, creating a warm and inviting ambiance. The space was filled with delicate touches and intricate details, each contributing to the overall sense of comfort and beauty.

In the living area, plush pink cushions adorned the cosy couch, inviting guests to sink into their softness. The room was adorned with tasteful decorations—a collection of art pieces, framed photographs capturing cherished memories, and potted plants adding a touch of life and freshness.

The space seamlessly transitioned into a charming dining area, with a petite table set for two. Delicate China, sparkling glassware, and a centrepiece of fresh flowers created an atmosphere of intimacy and elegance, perfect for sharing intimate conversations and meals.

Beyond the living area, a hallway led to the heart of the apartment—the bedroom. As Charlotte stepped inside, her eyes widened at the sight of a beautifully decorated sanctuary. The room emanated a serene aura, a haven where dreams could be woven and desires explored.

The centrepiece of the bedroom was a lavish, oversized bed—covered in soft pink satin sheets, adorned with plump pillows, and accompanied by a luxurious throw blanket. It beckoned Charlotte with its promise of comfort and intimacy, a space where passions could be ignited and pleasures indulged.

The walls of the bedroom were adorned with framed artwork, delicate lace curtains filtering the natural light that spilled through the windows. A vanity table, adorned with delicate perfumes, makeup brushes, and a mirror, stood in one corner—a place where Amelia undoubtedly prepared herself for the world with grace and poise.

As Charlotte explored the room further, she noticed a cosy reading nook, complete with a plush armchair and a bookshelf filled with an eclectic collection of literature. It was a corner of solitude, where Amelia could immerse herself in stories and escape to worlds beyond.

The girlish charm extended to the private bathroom—a space adorned with floral patterns, scented candles, and luxurious bath products. It promised moments of relaxation and self-care, where the outside world could be left behind, and indulgence in personal pleasures took centre stage.

In this girly haven, Charlotte felt a sense of intrigue and wonder. The apartment spoke volumes about Amelia's personality—a woman unafraid to embrace her femininity, surrounded by beauty and comfort.

As Charlotte's gaze settled on the inviting bed, she couldn't help but envision the possibilities that lay before them. The softness of the sheets, the glow of the candlelight, and the palpable connection between her and Amelia created an air of anticipation—a promise of a night where desires would be explored, boundaries pushed, and intimacy shared.

In the girly apartment, with its hues of pink and delicate touches, Charlotte and Amelia found themselves on the precipice of a journey into uncharted territory—a night where the exploration of their connection would unfold, and the depths of their desires would be unveiled in the embrace of the beautifully adorned bedroom.

As Charlotte and Amelia entered the confines of Amelia's girly haven, a palpable sense of anticipation filled the air. The soft hues of pink enveloped them, creating an atmosphere that exuded warmth and intimacy. They stood at the heart of the living space; their eyes locked in a silent agreement to explore the depths of their desires.

With a gentle touch, Charlotte reached out and took Amelia's hand in hers, their fingers intertwining in a dance of connection and intimacy. Their palms pressed against each other, radiating a warmth that mirrored the growing heat between them. The weight of their unspoken desires hung in the air, building a delicious tension that was ready to be unleashed.

Charlotte leaned in, her eyes sparkling with desire, and brushed her lips against Amelia's cheek, leaving a trail of delicate kisses. The sensation sent a shiver down Amelia's spine, igniting a fire that burned deep within her. Encouraged by Amelia's response, Charlotte's caresses grew bolder, her fingers tracing the contours of Amelia's face, memorizing every curve and feature.

Amelia's breath hitched as Charlotte's touch sent waves of pleasure coursing through her body. She closed her eyes, surrendering to the sensations that radiated from the gentle caresses. A soft moan escaped her lips, an invitation for Charlotte to explore further.

Feeling the power of Amelia's response, Charlotte's confidence soared. She moved her hand down Amelia's neck, her fingertips leaving a trail of electrifying sensations in their wake. With each touch, the intensity grew, a symphony of desire playing between them.

Emboldened by the chemistry that pulsed between them, Amelia reciprocated, her hands finding their way to Charlotte's waist. She pulled Charlotte closer, their bodies pressing against each other, an intimate embrace that spoke volumes. Their breaths mingled, and the heat between them intensified, a symphony of passion and longing reaching its crescendo.

Charlotte's lips found their way to Amelia's neck, trailing soft kisses along the sensitive skin. Her tongue teased, tasting the saltiness of desire that lingered there. The rhythm of their breaths quickened, syncing in a dance of shared anticipation.

Amelia's hands, guided by instinct, glided up Charlotte's back, her touch leaving a trail of goosebumps in its wake. She felt the warmth of Charlotte's skin beneath her fingertips, fuelling her desire to explore further. With a firm yet tender grip, Amelia pulled Charlotte closer, their bodies pressed together in a fervent embrace.

The world around them faded into oblivion as they surrendered to the intensity of the moment. They moved as one, their bodies swaying in a passionate rhythm, their hearts beating in sync. The girly haven bore witness to their desires, holding space for their exploration and connection.

With a surge of confidence, Charlotte's hands roamed Amelia's body, exploring every contour and curve. Fingers traced delicate patterns along Amelia's spine, sending shivers of pleasure cascading through her. Amelia's body responded to the touch, arching into Charlotte's caresses, a silent plea for more.

Their lips finally met in a searing kiss—a collision of passion and longing that left them breathless. Their tongues danced in a sensual tango, their mouths melding together in a harmony that expressed their shared desire. It was a kiss that conveyed all the unspoken words, the yearning, and the hunger that had built between them.

The gentle sway of the music playing in the background mirrored the rhythm of their bodies, heightening the sensory experience. The world outside ceased to exist as their connection deepened, their bodies entwined in an intimate dance of exploration and pleasure.

Clothes fell away, revealing the vulnerability and beauty that lay beneath. Their bodies, now fully exposed, became canvases on which desires were painted. The girly haven embraced them, providing a safe space where inhibitions dissolved, and passions ran free.

Laying on the bed adorned with soft pink satin sheets, their bodies intertwined, they explored each other with a hunger that only grew with each touch. Fingertips traced along every curve, lips caressed every inch of exposed skin, and breaths mingled in a symphony of pleasure.

As the night unfolded, Charlotte and Amelia surrendered to the depths of their desires, igniting a fire that burned brighter with every intimate connection. They discovered the power of vulnerability and trust, exploring the landscape of pleasure with a shared understanding that transcended words.

Their bodies moved in perfect harmony, a choreography of desire that built and built until it crashed like a wave, engulfing them in waves of ecstasy. In the girly haven, time stood still as they lost themselves in the passion, their hearts and bodies merging into one.

Afterward, they lay entwined, bodies glistening with sweat, and hearts still racing with the echoes of their shared pleasure. The girly haven embraced them in a tender embrace, providing a space for them to bask in the afterglow of their intimate exploration.

In the stillness of the moment, Charlotte and Amelia exchanged soft, lingering kisses, their fingers intertwined. The depth of their connection had blossomed further, their desires explored and affirmed. Their souls had danced together, and in that girly haven, they found solace, understanding, and a love that defied expectations.

As they drifted off to sleep, cradled in each other's arms, the girly haven whispered promises of future adventures, inviting them to continue exploring the depths of their desires, knowing that their connection was a tapestry that would be woven with tenderness, trust, and a shared sense of liberation.

In that moment, they realized that their journey had only just begun—a journey that celebrated the vast spectrum of love, where they would continue to dive into the uncharted waters of desire, guided by the whispers of their hearts and the embrace of the girly haven that had witnessed the blossoming of their passion.

Amelia and Charlotte lay side by side, their bodies still basking in the glow of their intimate connection. The room was hushed, the air heavy with a mixture of contentment and vulnerability. With a gentle touch, Amelia reached out and brushed a strand of hair away from Charlotte's face, her voice filled with tenderness and affection.

Amelia: "Charlotte, that was... incredible. I can't put into words how much it meant to me. I've never experienced such a deep connection with another woman before."

Charlotte turned to face Amelia, a soft smile gracing her lips as she mirrored the affection in her voice.

Charlotte: "Amelia, it was beyond anything I could have imagined. This was my first time with a woman, and I'm grateful that it was with you. The connection we share, the tenderness and respect we've shown each other—it's truly special."

Amelia's eyes gleamed with a mixture of joy and relief, reassured by Charlotte's response.

Amelia: "I'm so glad to hear that, Charlotte. This was also my first time with another woman, and I couldn't have asked for a more beautiful and respectful experience. There's a certain magic that comes with exploring new aspects of our desires, and I'm grateful that we could share this together."

Charlotte nodded, her fingers delicately tracing patterns along Amelia's arm.

Charlotte: "Absolutely. It's empowering to embrace our desires and step into the unknown, without any regrets or judgment. Our connection tonight has reaffirmed my belief that love knows no boundaries, and pleasure can be found in the most unexpected places."

Amelia's gaze softened; her voice filled with genuine sincerity.

Amelia: "You're right, Charlotte. Love and pleasure have a way of defying societal norms and expectations. Tonight, we've shown each other that there's beauty in embracing our authentic selves, even if it means venturing into uncharted territory. Our experience was romantic, respectful, and filled with shared pleasure."

They lay there, their bodies entwined, savouring the intimate moments they had just shared. The room enveloped them in a bubble of vulnerability and trust, allowing them to open up and express their feelings without fear of judgment.

Charlotte broke the silence, her voice gentle yet filled with curiosity.

Charlotte: "Amelia, may I ask how you're feeling now? This experience, this connection we've forged—it's a profound step on our personal journeys. Are you content? Is there anything you need?"

Amelia turned to face Charlotte, her expression warm and sincere.

Amelia: "Charlotte, I couldn't be more content. This experience has surpassed any expectations I had. Being with you, sharing this intimate connection, has been a gift. And to know that we both feel this way, without regret, is truly special. As for what I need, being in your presence and feeling the depth of our connection is all I could ask for in this moment."

A soft smile played on Charlotte's lips as she squeezed Amelia's hand.

Charlotte: "Amelia, I'm so grateful for your presence in my life. This journey we're embarking on together is uncharted, but knowing that we're supporting and understanding each other makes it feel like the most natural path to follow. Our connection is a testament to the beauty of exploration and the limitless possibilities of love."

Their eyes met, and in that moment, they knew they had found not only a physical connection but a kindred spirit. They were companions on a voyage of self-discovery, and their shared experiences would continue to shape their understanding of love, desire, and the complexities of the human heart.

In the gentle embrace of the afterglow, they understood that their experience together was not just a fleeting moment, but a stepping stone towards a deeper understanding of themselves and the infinite potential that lay within their connection.

As they lay there, hearts entwined, they felt a sense of liberation and empowerment. They had embraced their desires, shattered societal expectations, and allowed love to guide them towards a more authentic expression of themselves. Their journey had just begun, and with every shared experience, they would continue to navigate the uncharted waters of pleasure, love, and self-discovery together.

• • • •

AS THE MORNING SUNLIGHT filtered through the curtains, Charlotte felt a sense of warmth and contentment wash over her. She gently disentangled herself from Amelia's embrace, pressing a tender kiss on her lips before getting ready to leave.

Charlotte: "Amelia, thank you for everything. Last night was truly special, and I'm grateful for the connection we shared. I have some things to attend to today, but I hope we can continue our conversation soon."

Amelia's eyes sparkled with a mix of fondness and understanding as she reached out to caress Charlotte's cheek.

Amelia: "Charlotte, you've brought so much light into my life. I cherish the moments we've shared, and I look forward to our continued connection. Take your time, follow your path, and know that I'll be here whenever you're ready."

A soft smile graced Charlotte's lips as she nodded in appreciation, savouring the lingering connection between them.

Charlotte: "Thank you, Amelia. Your understanding and support mean the world to me. Until we meet again."

With a final glance, Charlotte bid farewell to Amelia and stepped out of the apartment, the memories of their time together still fresh in her mind. As she walked away, a mixture of gratitude and anticipation filled her heart, ready to face the new chapter that awaited her.

Chapter 5 A New Dawn: Exploring Truths and Embracing Courage

••••

AFTER LEAVING AMELIA'S apartment, Charlotte made her way back home, her thoughts swirling with a mix of emotions. As she stepped into the familiarity of her house, she felt a sense of calm wash over her. The warm water of the shower embraced her body, cleansing both her skin and her mind.

Under the soothing cascade, Charlotte's thoughts turned to Amelia and Mark. She couldn't deny the impact they had both made on her life in such a short span of time. Each connection was unique and held its own significance, stirring different desires within her.

As the water cascaded over her, Charlotte's mind wandered through the memories of her encounters with Amelia and the exhilarating moments shared with Mark. She recognized that she had a need to explore both connections further, to delve deeper into the possibilities that lay before her.

With a renewed sense of spontaneity and a desire to follow the calling of her soul, Charlotte made a decision. She would reach out to Mark and arrange to meet him again, to continue the conversation that had been left unfinished.

Drying herself off, she wrapped a towel around her body and made her way to her room. There, she rummaged through her closet, selecting an outfit that reflected her confidence and curiosity. With a touch of excitement, she slipped into a comfortable yet stylish ensemble, envisioning the encounter that awaited her.

As the clock ticked closer to lunchtime, Charlotte gathered her belongings and made her way to the harbour. The sound of seagulls and the gentle sway of the boats greeted her as she approached the dock. Her heart fluttered with a mix of anticipation and nervousness as she sought out Mark's boat, its familiar presence standing tall against the sparkling blue backdrop of the water.

Taking a deep breath, Charlotte climbed aboard the boat, the wooden deck beneath her feet grounding her. The sun kissed her skin, casting a warm glow over her face. She glanced around, taking in the sights and sounds of the harbour, as she eagerly awaited Mark's arrival.

In that moment, with the sea breeze caressing her cheeks and the promise of new possibilities on the horizon, Charlotte knew she was following her heart's calling. The spontaneity of her soul propelled her forward, embracing the uncertainty and the potential for meaningful connections.

As she waited, a sense of empowerment surged through her. She had chosen to be true to herself, to explore the depths of her desires and the possibilities that lay within. Whether it was Amelia or Mark, or perhaps even someone entirely unexpected, Charlotte was ready to embrace the connections that awaited her, to embark on a journey that would lead her closer to her authentic self.

With her heart filled with anticipation, Charlotte waited for Mark, her mind open to the adventure that awaited her. She was ready to engage in the spontaneity of her soul, to navigate the uncharted waters of love, and to discover the beautiful complexities of connection that lay ahead.

Dressed in a stylish mini skirt and with a touch of waterproof makeup enhancing her natural beauty, Charlotte exuded confidence and anticipation. She hopped into her car, the engine purring to life as she embarked on her journey to Mark's boat.

The wind gently tousled her hair as she navigated the streets, her mind filled with a mix of excitement and curiosity. The drive seemed to pass in a blur as she eagerly anticipated the moment she would reunite with Mark.

Arriving at the harbour, Charlotte's eyes scanned the scene until they landed on Mark's boat. A surge of relief and joy filled her as she spotted him on deck, his presence commanding and welcoming.

With a skip in her step, Charlotte made her way toward the boat, the sound of her heels echoing against the wooden pier. As she reached the deck, Mark's face lit up with a big, warm smile that mirrored her own.

Mark: "Charlotte! I'm thrilled to see you again. You look absolutely stunning."

Charlotte's smile widened at his genuine compliment, her heart fluttering in response to his warm reception.

Charlotte: "Thank you, Mark. It's wonderful to see you too. I couldn't resist the opportunity to continue our conversation and spend some time together."

Mark extended his hand, inviting Charlotte to step aboard the boat. With a graceful movement, she accepted, feeling a sense of anticipation building between them.

Mark: "I'm honoured that you chose to visit me. The timing couldn't be more perfect. Let's make the most of this time together."

As they settled onto the boat's deck, the sun cast a golden glow around them, creating an ambiance that felt both intimate and inviting. Their conversation flowed effortlessly, each word deepening their connection as they shared stories, dreams, and aspirations.

With every passing moment, Charlotte found herself drawn to Mark's charisma and the genuine interest he showed in getting to know her. Their chemistry was undeniable, a magnetic force that pulled them closer, sparking a newfound excitement within Charlotte's heart.

As they laughed and shared anecdotes, their conversations occasionally dipped into more profound topics, exploring their desires, passions, and the complexities of love. Mark's ability to listen and respond with genuine empathy only deepened the bond they were forming.

As the afternoon sun began its descent, casting a warm hue over the harbour, Charlotte felt a sense of contentment settle within her. She had taken a leap of faith, allowing her spontaneity to guide her, and it had led her to this moment of connection and possibility.

Their time together on the boat felt like a glimpse into a future filled with exploration, shared experiences, and the potential for a meaningful connection. Charlotte was grateful for the spontaneity that had brought them together, and she looked forward to discovering where their journey would lead.

With the gentle rocking of the boat and the rhythm of their conversation, Charlotte felt a growing sense of trust and excitement. In Mark's presence, she knew that she could be true to herself, unafraid to explore her desires and embrace the spontaneity of her soul.

As the sun dipped below the horizon, casting a breath-taking display of colours across the sky, Charlotte and Mark continued to share laughter, stories, and dreams. The possibilities ahead seemed endless, and they were ready to embark on this new chapter together, with open hearts and a shared enthusiasm for the connections that awaited them.

Mark's invitation to explore the bedroom of his luxurious boat ignited a sense of intrigue and anticipation within Charlotte. As they made their way to the bedroom, Charlotte's eyes widened in awe as the door swung open, revealing a space that exuded elegance and comfort.

The bedroom was a sanctuary nestled within the heart of the boat. Soft, dimmed lighting created an intimate ambiance, casting a warm glow over the room. The walls were adorned with intricately designed wood panelling, evoking a sense of timeless beauty.

The centrepiece of the room was a lavish king-sized bed, adorned with plush pillows and a sumptuous duvet. The sheets were silky-smooth, inviting Charlotte to sink into their embrace. The headboard featured an exquisite tufted design, adding a touch of sophistication to the space.

A sleek, polished wooden floor stretched beneath their feet, accentuated by a plush area rug that provided a cosy space to step onto when leaving the bed. Large windows framed by delicate curtains offered glimpses of the breath-taking views outside, allowing the gentle breeze and the distant sounds of the water to serenade the room.

The room was thoughtfully designed with comfort and relaxation in mind. A small seating area, complete with a plush armchair and a side table, provided a cosy corner for intimate conversations. Soft, decorative accents adorned the room, adding a personal touch and infusing a sense of serenity.

As Charlotte stepped further into the room, she noticed a spacious bathroom, boasting sleek marble countertops, a luxurious bathtub, and a spacious shower. The elegance of the fixtures and the attention to detail in the design spoke to the opulence of the boat.

Mark gestured toward the bed, his eyes filled with a mix of desire and genuine care.

Mark: "Charlotte, welcome to my private haven. This room holds the promise of comfort, intimacy, and shared moments. I invite you to explore this space with me, to create memories that will linger long after we leave this boat."

Charlotte's heart quickened at Mark's words, her gaze shifting between the inviting bed and his captivating eyes. She felt a surge of excitement and trust in the connection they were forging.

Charlotte: "Mark, this room is simply stunning. It reflects the elegance and thoughtfulness you've shown throughout our time together. I'm ready to embrace the intimacy and the possibilities that await us here."

Mark's smile deepened, a blend of desire and respect shining in his eyes.

Mark: "Thank you, Charlotte. It's important to me that you feel comfortable and cherished in this space. Together, we'll create a journey filled with mutual respect, passion, and exploration."

With a shared understanding and a magnetic pull drawing them closer, Mark and Charlotte stepped toward the bed, their hearts brimming with anticipation. In this haven of luxury and desire, they were ready to surrender to the possibilities that lay ahead, embracing the intimacy and connection that awaited them within the confines of the boat's elegant bedroom.

As Charlotte settled onto the luxurious bed, she could feel a mix of emotions swirling within her. The memory of her intimate connection with Amelia still lingered, intertwining with the growing desire that Mark's touch ignited. She looked into his eyes, a combination of curiosity and vulnerability reflecting in her gaze.

Sensing the depth of Charlotte's emotions, Mark approached her with a gentle and attentive demeanour. His hand, warm and inviting, reached out to caress her cheek, tracing delicate patterns along her skin. The electric touch sent a shiver down Charlotte's spine, amplifying her anticipation.

Their eyes locked, communicating a silent understanding between them. In that moment, the connection they shared seemed to transcend time and space, a testament to the complexities of desire and the power of human connection.

Mark's touch gradually wandered, exploring the contours of Charlotte's body with an exquisite tenderness. His fingertips traced the curve of her neck, the slope of her shoulder, and the softness of her waist, leaving a trail of fire in their wake. Charlotte's breath quickened, her body responding instinctively to the delicate dance of pleasure that Mark orchestrated.

In the midst of their intimate encounter, Charlotte found herself surrendering to the sensations that coursed through her. The intertwining of pleasure and vulnerability created a tapestry of emotions that both exhilarated and comforted her. She marvelled at the fluidity of desire and the capacity of her own heart to hold space for the connections she was exploring.

As Mark's lips found hers in a passionate kiss, Charlotte's world became consumed by the intensity of their union. The taste and warmth of their mingling breaths, the caress of their tongues, and the rhythm of their bodies moving in unison kindled a fire that burned brighter with each passing moment.

In this intimate exchange, Charlotte felt a profound connection with Mark—a connection that existed in its own right, separate from her experience with Amelia. It was a testament to the depth and complexity of human desire, and the capacity of the heart to hold multiple connections, each unique and significant in its own way.

As their bodies moved together, the boundaries between them blurred, dissolving into a sea of shared pleasure and exploration. The sensations that rippled through Charlotte's body were both familiar and entirely new, a testament to the power of the present moment and the depths of her own desires.

As the intensity of their encounter built, Charlotte found herself embracing the incredible sensations that Mark evoked within her. The juxtaposition of her experiences with Amelia and Mark, though distinct, created a tapestry of self-discovery and connection that shaped her understanding of her own desires and the capacity for love within her heart.

In the sanctuary of the elegant bedroom, Charlotte and Mark revealed in the beauty of their intimate connection. Their exploration transcended any preconceived notions or expectations, offering a space for vulnerability, pleasure, and a deepening bond between two souls willing to embrace the unexpected.

As their bodies intertwined, their shared experience became a testament to the complexity and fluidity of desire. In that moment, Charlotte surrendered to the overwhelming sensations, allowing herself to be fully present and open to the incredible intimacy that Mark offered.

In the embrace of the moment, Charlotte discovered that she was capable of embracing the diverse connections that life presented, savouring the unique experiences that each brought. The layers of her desires unfurled, intertwining her experiences with both Amelia and Mark, revealing the intricacies and nuances that made up the tapestry of her own journey of self-discovery and love.

As the intensity of their intimate encounter began to subside, Charlotte found herself caught in a moment of vulnerability and introspection. The raw emotions that had surged through her during their passionate exchange had left her with a sense of unease. She looked into Mark's eyes, her voice trembling with a mix of shame and curiosity.

Charlotte: "Mark, I... I need to talk to you about something. During our intimacy just now, I found myself... I don't know how to say it, but I had these uncontrollable screams. It's never happened to me before, and I feel a bit ashamed."

Mark's expression softened, and he reached out to gently stroke Charlotte's cheek, his eyes filled with understanding and reassurance.

Mark: "Charlotte, there's no need to feel ashamed. In fact, I'm glad that our connection evoked such a powerful response in you. It's a testament to the intensity of the moment and the deep connection we share. Your uninhibited expression of pleasure is beautiful, and it's completely natural to experience new sensations and responses."

Charlotte's eyes widened as she absorbed Mark's words, a mix of relief and acceptance washing over her.

Charlotte: "You're not... upset or put off by it?"

Mark shook his head, a genuine smile gracing his lips.

Mark: "Absolutely not, Charlotte. I embrace and celebrate your authenticity and the uninhibited expression of your desires. It's a sign of trust and openness between us. Each connection we have is unique, and it's these moments of exploration that allow us to learn more about ourselves and our desires."

As Mark's words sank in, Charlotte began to realize the significance of her experience and the journey she was on. The shame that had once clouded her thoughts began to dissipate, replaced by a newfound understanding and acceptance of her own desires.

Charlotte: "I'm beginning to understand that my desires are fluid and ever-evolving. The connection I have with you and the experiences I've had with both men and women have shown me that I have the capacity to embrace the beauty of both worlds. It's about honouring my authentic self and allowing my heart to lead the way."

Mark's eyes sparkled with a mix of admiration and encouragement; his voice filled with support.

Mark: "Charlotte, you're on a beautiful journey of self-discovery, and it's incredible to witness. Embracing the diversity of your desires is a courageous and empowering choice. By honouring and exploring the connections that resonate with you, you're forging a path that is true to your authentic self."

As Charlotte absorbed Mark's words, a sense of clarity and acceptance settled within her. She realized that her journey would be one of embracing the complexities of her desires, alternating between connections with both men and women as they felt right for her at different times.

In this newfound understanding, Charlotte felt a deep sense of liberation and gratitude. She was grateful for the experiences that had brought her to this moment, grateful for the connection she shared with Mark, and grateful for the opportunity to explore the depths of her desires with an open heart.

With their conversation, a weight had been lifted, and a newfound sense of empowerment guided Charlotte's path forward. She understood that her journey would be unique, shaped by her own desires and the connections that would come her way. She embraced the beauty of fluidity and the freedom to explore love in all its diverse forms.

In the arms of Mark, Charlotte felt a renewed sense of self-acceptance and a burgeoning excitement for the adventures that awaited her. The alternating embrace of both men and women would be her path, a path illuminated by self-discovery, connection, and the unending possibilities of love.

Chapter 6 Embracing the Dance of Connections

During the following month, Charlotte found herself navigating the delicate dance of connections with both Mark and Amelia. Unbeknownst to either of them, Charlotte had embraced polyamory and was seeking fulfilment in the unique bonds she shared with each of them.

Her time with Mark was filled with adventurous outings and passionate moments. They explored new places together, from picturesque hikes in the mountains to romantic dinners at hidden gems in the city. The chemistry between them was undeniable, and their connection continued to deepen with each passing day. Charlotte revelled in the excitement and passion that Mark brought into her life, cherishing the moments they shared.

Meanwhile, her encounters with Amelia were equally transformative. They delved into profound conversations, sharing their deepest fears, dreams, and experiences. Amelia's tender touch and understanding nature provided a sense of solace and emotional connection that Charlotte had longed for. With Amelia, Charlotte discovered the beauty of vulnerability and the power of shared experiences.

Throughout this month, Charlotte skilfully balanced her time between Mark and Amelia, ensuring that each relationship received the attention and care it deserved. She dedicated herself to being fully present in their presence, appreciating the unique qualities that made each connection special.

While Mark and Amelia were unaware of each other's existence in Charlotte's life, she found solace in the knowledge that she was living her truth and embracing the fulfilling connections that polyamory allowed. She revelled in the beauty of her multi-faceted desires, finding joy in the diversity of experiences and the ability to forge deep connections with multiple individuals.

This month became a time of self-discovery and growth for Charlotte. She began to understand the intricacies of her own heart, realizing that love had no boundaries and that fulfilment could be found in the authentic exploration of connections.

In the moments shared with Mark and Amelia, Charlotte felt a sense of wholeness. Each relationship brought forth unique qualities and awakened different aspects of her being. She embraced the complexities of love, understanding that fulfilment could be found in the connections that resonated deeply with her soul.

As the month unfolded, Charlotte's understanding of polyamory deepened. She began to reflect on the beauty of navigating multiple connections, appreciating the diversity of experiences and the capacity of the heart to hold love for more than one person.

While the path ahead was filled with uncertainties, Charlotte felt empowered and fulfilled. She had embraced her desires, honouring the connections that brought her joy and allowing her heart to guide her in the exploration of love.

In the intricate tapestry of her relationships with Mark and Amelia, Charlotte discovered a newfound sense of authenticity, liberation, and personal growth. She understood that her journey would continue to evolve, and she welcomed the endless possibilities that lay before her.

As the month drew to a close, Charlotte marvelled at the profound impact that embracing polyamory had on her life. She knew that this was just the beginning, and that her path would be one of continual exploration, connection, and self-discovery.

In the privacy of her home, Charlotte found solace and a safe space to delve into her thoughts and feelings. As she sat in reflection, her newfound self-confidence radiated through her being. She had embraced polyamory, embracing the truth of her desires and the fulfilment that came from nurturing connections with both Mark and Amelia.

Taking a deep breath, Charlotte spoke aloud, addressing herself as she contemplated the path ahead.

Charlotte: "I have come to understand the importance of authenticity and honesty in my relationships. I have chosen to embrace the beauty of loving multiple people, and now it is time to face the truth and communicate this to both Mark and Amelia. It may not be an easy conversation, but I owe it to myself and to them to be open, transparent, and true."

With each word, Charlotte felt her resolve strengthening. She recognized the significance of her decision to maintain both connections, realizing that choosing one over the other would not bring her the fulfilment she sought.

Charlotte: "I will not choose between them. I will honour the connections I have formed with Mark and Amelia, acknowledging their individuality and the unique bonds we share. It is through embracing both connections that I can truly honour my own desires and navigate this journey of love and self-discovery."

As she spoke these words, a sense of freedom washed over Charlotte. She knew that this path required courage and open communication, but she was prepared to face the challenges that lay ahead.

Charlotte: "I will approach these conversations with love, respect, and a willingness to listen. I will share my truth with Mark and Amelia, allowing them the space to process and express their own thoughts and emotions. Together, we will navigate the complexities of our connections, embracing the possibilities that lie before us."

With a renewed sense of determination, Charlotte began to consider the reasons why she needed to be truthful with both Mark and Amelia. She understood that honesty was the foundation upon which trust and authenticity were built.

Charlotte: "telling the truth will allow me to maintain the integrity of our relationships. It will foster an environment of trust and open communication, creating a space where our connections can thrive. It will also give Mark and Amelia the opportunity to make informed decisions about their own desires and boundaries."

As she considered the potential outcomes, Charlotte acknowledged the possibility of difficult conversations and challenging emotions. Yet, she also recognized the potential for growth, understanding, and the deepening of their connections.

Charlotte: "By embracing vulnerability and speaking my truth, I am opening the door for growth, both individually and within our relationships. We may face moments of uncertainty and discomfort, but it is through these challenges that we have the opportunity to learn, evolve, and strengthen the bonds we share."

With her thoughts clarified and her commitment solidified, Charlotte made a vow to herself. She would embark on the journey of truth and open communication, knowing that it would require courage, empathy, and an unwavering commitment to honesty.

Charlotte: "I will hold space for Mark and Amelia's responses, allowing them to express their thoughts and emotions without judgment. I will honour their individual journeys and decisions, even if they differ from my own. Through this process, I will remain true to myself, embracing the beauty of love in all its diverse forms."

With her self-reflection complete, Charlotte felt a renewed sense of purpose and determination. She knew that the conversations ahead would shape the trajectory of their relationships, but she also knew that she was ready to face whatever came her way. In her commitment to honesty and authenticity, she would navigate the complexities of polyamory with grace and integrity, remaining steadfast in her pursuit of love and self-discovery.

Chapter 7 Unveiling the Truth

A melia sat across from Charlotte in a cosy coffee shop, completely unaware of the revelation that was about to unfold. Charlotte took a deep breath, her heart pounding with a mix of nervousness and determination. This conversation would be a pivotal moment in their connection, one that would require courage and vulnerability.

Charlotte: "Amelia, there's something important I need to share with you. It's about our connection and the journey I've been on."

Amelia looked at Charlotte, her eyes filled with curiosity and concern. She reached out, placing a reassuring hand on Charlotte's, silently encouraging her to continue.

Amelia: "What is it, Charlotte? You can tell me anything. We've built a strong bond, and I'm here to listen."

Charlotte took a moment to gather her thoughts, knowing that the words she was about to speak would have a profound impact on their relationship.

Charlotte: "Amelia, over the past few months, I've come to understand and embrace a part of myself that I hadn't fully explored before. I have realized that I am polyamorous, meaning that I have the capacity and desire to love and connect with multiple people simultaneously."

Amelia's eyes widened with a mix of surprise and curiosity. She listened intently; her gaze fixed on Charlotte.

Amelia: "Polyamory... I've heard of it, but I'm not sure I fully understand. Can you explain it to me?"

Charlotte nodded, appreciating Amelia's willingness to learn and engage in an open conversation.

Charlotte: "Of course. Polyamory is the practice of having multiple loving, consensual relationships at the same time, with the knowledge and consent of all involved. It's about fostering connections with multiple individuals and nurturing each bond individually. It's important for me to be honest with you because I value our connection deeply."

Amelia took a moment to process the information, her brow furrowing in contemplation. She took a sip of her coffee before responding.

Amelia: "Thank you for being honest with me, Charlotte. This is new territory for me, but I appreciate your openness. Does this mean that you have other connections besides ours?"

Charlotte nodded, understanding the weight of her words and the potential impact they could have on Amelia.

Charlotte: "Yes, Amelia. I have also formed a connection with another person, a man named Mark. I value both of these connections deeply, and it is important for me to be authentic and transparent with each of you."

Amelia took a moment to let the information sink in, her expression thoughtful as she considered the implications.

Amelia: "I must admit, this is unexpected. But I value our connection too, Charlotte. I appreciate the honesty and trust you've shown in sharing this with me. While it may take time for me to fully understand and navigate the complexities of polyamory, I'm willing to explore this with an open mind."

Relief washed over Charlotte as she listened to Amelia's response. The acceptance and willingness to engage in an open dialogue eased her fears and brought a sense of hope.

Charlotte: "Thank you, Amelia. Your understanding and open-mindedness mean a great deal to me. I want to ensure that our connection remains strong and that we have the space to explore our bond in a way that feels comfortable for both of us. I'm committed to open communication and to respecting your boundaries."

Amelia smiled warmly, her hand reaching across the table to hold Charlotte's.

Amelia: "Charlotte, our connection has been a source of joy and growth for me. I believe that with honest communication, empathy, and mutual understanding, we can navigate the complexities of polyamory together. Let's continue to explore our bond, keeping our lines of communication open as we learn more about ourselves and each other."

Charlotte's heart swelled with gratitude, relieved to have shared her truth and to have found acceptance in Amelia's response.

Charlotte: "Thank you, Amelia. Your support and willingness to embark on this journey mean the world to me. Let's navigate this new chapter together, honouring our connection and embracing the opportunities for growth and fulfilment that lie ahead."

As they sat there, hand in hand, a new sense of unity and understanding blossomed between Charlotte and Amelia. Their connection had deepened through vulnerability and open communication, paving the way for a shared exploration of love, self-discovery, and the beauty of polyamory.

As Charlotte left the coffee shop, she felt a mix of nerves and determination as she prepared to reveal the truth to Mark. The support and understanding she had received from Amelia gave her an extra boost of confidence. She knew that being honest and authentic with Mark was crucial for the future of their connection.

Arriving at their agreed-upon meeting spot, Charlotte spotted Mark waiting, his expression a blend of anticipation and curiosity. She approached him with a newfound sense of clarity, ready to share her truth.

Charlotte: "Mark, there's something important I need to discuss with you. It's about our connection and the journey I've been on."

Mark's brows furrowed slightly, his eyes narrowing with a mix of surprise and intrigue.

Mark: "What is it, Charlotte? You seem serious. I'm all ears."

Charlotte took a deep breath, drawing strength from the support she had received from Amelia. She knew that the upcoming conversation would shape the trajectory of her relationship with Mark.

Charlotte: "I've come to understand that I am polyamorous. It means that I have the capacity and desire to love and connect with multiple people simultaneously. I value our connection deeply, and it's important for me to be honest with you."

Mark's initial surprise was quickly replaced by a thoughtful expression as he processed Charlotte's revelation. He took a moment to gather his thoughts before responding.

Mark: "I appreciate your honesty, Charlotte. It's not something I expected to hear, but I respect your courage in sharing this with me. Can you help me understand what this means for our connection?"

Charlotte nodded, appreciating Mark's open-mindedness and willingness to engage in the conversation.

Charlotte: "Being polyamorous means that I am open to forming connections with multiple individuals, including you and someone else I've grown close to. I value what we have together, and I want to ensure that our connection remains strong while also exploring the potential of other relationships."

Mark listened attentively, his expression a mix of curiosity and contemplation.

Mark: "I won't deny that this is a new concept for me, but I admire your commitment to honesty and transparency. It's clear that our connection is special, and I believe in open communication and understanding. While I may need some time to fully grasp the intricacies of polyamory, I'm willing to explore this with you."

Relief washed over Charlotte as she heard Mark's response. The acceptance and willingness to engage in a conversation about polyamory opened up a realm of possibilities for their connection.

Charlotte: "Thank you, Mark. Your understanding and willingness to embark on this journey mean a great deal to me. It's important for me to ensure that our connection is built on trust, open communication, and respect for each other's boundaries."

Mark smiled, his eyes reflecting a mix of admiration and determination.

Mark: "Charlotte, our connection has been filled with joy, laughter, and shared experiences. While this may be uncharted territory for me, I believe that love is a complex and ever-evolving journey. Let's continue to explore our bond, embracing the opportunities for growth and fulfilment that lie ahead."

With a shared sense of understanding and a commitment to open communication, Charlotte and Mark embraced the unknown. The path before them was one of discovery, exploration, and a deepening connection rooted in acceptance and trust.

As they continued their conversation, Charlotte felt a renewed sense of gratitude for the connections she had forged. She understood that being true to herself and embracing polyamory allowed her to navigate the intricacies of love in a way that honoured her desires and nurtured the connections she held dear.

In this moment of vulnerability and acceptance, Charlotte and Mark set forth on a shared journey of growth and self-discovery, guided by open communication and an unwavering commitment to building a connection that celebrated the beauty of their individualities and the possibility of multiple loves.

Mark was curious about Amelia and as he enjoys ex he asked directly to Charlotte if Amelia would accept to make love with him. Charlotte was surprised but not shocked by the idea.

Charlotte's eyes widened slightly at Mark's unexpected request, her surprise mingling with a hint of intrigue. The directness of his question caught her off guard, yet she appreciated his openness and curiosity.

Charlotte took a moment to gather her thoughts before responding, considering the potential implications and the dynamics between the three of them.

Charlotte: "Mark, I appreciate your honesty and openness about your curiosity. However, it's important for me to approach this situation with respect for Amelia and her boundaries. While I cannot speak for her, I believe that it would be best for us to have a conversation about this as a group, ensuring that everyone involved has a voice and the opportunity to express their feelings and desires."

Mark nodded, acknowledging the importance of open communication and consent.

Mark: "You're right, Charlotte. It's essential that we approach this situation with respect and consideration for everyone involved. I would never want to jeopardize our connection or create any discomfort between us. Let's discuss this as a group and ensure that everyone's feelings and boundaries are respected."

Charlotte felt a sense of relief and reassurance in Mark's response. She appreciated his willingness to prioritize open communication and consent, recognizing the importance of navigating the situation with care and respect for all parties involved.

Together, they made a decision to engage in a conversation that would include Amelia, creating a space for open dialogue and understanding. They understood that the outcome of the discussion would depend on Amelia's feelings and comfort level, and that the priority was to maintain the trust and respect within their connections.

With a renewed sense of purpose, Charlotte and Mark set out to communicate with Amelia, seeking her input and perspective on the matter. They understood that their journey of exploring polyamory would require ongoing communication, honesty, and the willingness to navigate new experiences together while honouring each other's boundaries.

As they embarked on this new chapter, their shared commitment to open communication and consent would guide them in exploring the complexities and possibilities of their connections. It was through these conversations that they would forge a path that celebrated the beauty of love, authenticity, and the unique dynamics that can arise in polyamorous relationships.

The phone rang, interrupting the stillness of the room. Charlotte's heart skipped a beat as she saw Amelia's name flashing on the screen. She picked up the call, her voice filled with anticipation.

Charlotte: "Amelia, it's great to hear from you. How are you?"

Amelia's voice carried a mix of curiosity and excitement as she spoke.

Amelia: "Charlotte, I've been doing some thinking since our conversation earlier. I appreciate your honesty, and I must admit, I'm intrigued. But before we delve deeper into this journey, I want to know where Mark stands on the idea of polyamory."

Charlotte glanced at Mark, a knowing look passing between them. She relayed Amelia's question to Mark, who listened intently before responding.

Mark: "Amelia, I appreciate your curiosity and your desire for open communication. I've been reflecting on polyamory since Charlotte shared her truth with me. I believe that it's important for us to have an open and honest conversation about this as a group, where we can all express our thoughts, feelings, and boundaries. Would you be open to joining us for a Sunday lunch, where we can discuss this further?"

There was a brief pause on the line as Amelia considered Mark's proposal. The idea of a face-to-face conversation seemed to resonate with her.

Amelia: "I think that's a fair and respectful approach, Mark. A Sunday lunch sounds like a perfect opportunity for us to discuss our feelings, concerns, and desires. I appreciate your willingness to engage in this conversation, and I'm open to exploring the possibilities that polyamory holds for us."

Charlotte felt a sense of relief wash over her as Amelia expressed her openness to the idea. She admired the willingness of both Mark and Amelia to engage in open dialogue and create a space for shared understanding.

Charlotte: "Thank you both for your openness and willingness to explore this together. I believe that the Sunday lunch will provide us with the opportunity to listen to one another, ask questions, and ensure that we all feel comfortable moving forward. I will organize the lunch and find a suitable venue where we can have a private and intimate conversation."

With the date set for their meeting, a sense of anticipation filled the air. Each of them understood the importance of this gathering and the potential for growth and understanding that it held. They approached it with a shared commitment to honesty, respect, and the exploration of their connections within the framework of polyamory.

As Charlotte hung up the phone, she felt a renewed sense of hope and excitement. The path ahead was still uncertain, but she knew that they were embarking on a journey that would shape their connections in profound ways. With open hearts and open minds, they would navigate the complexities of polyamory, honouring their desires, and creating a foundation of trust and communication.

The Sunday lunch would be a pivotal moment, where they would come together to share their thoughts, fears, and aspirations. It would be a space where their individualities and desires could be expressed and heard, laying the groundwork for a future that embraced the beauty of multiple connections and the possibilities of love in all its diverse forms.

Chapter 8 The Convergence of Hearts and Minds

The Sunday arrived, and Charlotte's house was bustling with energy and anticipation. She had meticulously prepared a delicious lunch for Mark and Amelia, eager to create an atmosphere of comfort and warmth for this pivotal meeting. The table was adorned with a crisp, white tablecloth and adorned with delicate floral arrangements. The soft glow of candles added a touch of intimacy to the scene.

In the living room, where they would gather for their conversation, Charlotte had arranged plush seating, ensuring that each person would feel at ease and able to express themselves openly. The room exuded a cosy charm, with warm earth tones and soft lighting that created an inviting ambiance.

As Charlotte put the finishing touches on the table, her hands trembled with a mixture of nervousness and excitement. She had been longing for this moment, hoping that Mark and Amelia would connect and find common ground. Her desire for their harmonious interaction fuelled her nervous energy, as she yearned for a deep understanding and acceptance among them.

Charlotte paced the room, her heart racing, as she envisioned the possibilities of the conversation to come. She wanted nothing more than for Amelia and Mark to see the genuine love and respect she held for both of them. She hoped they would embrace the concept of polyamory, recognizing its potential for growth and fulfilment.

Her nerves were accompanied by a sense of hope, intermingled with the underlying fear of the unknown. She knew that their shared journey could unfold in myriad ways, and it was this uncertainty that both thrilled and unsettled her.

As the time drew near, Charlotte took a deep breath, centring herself in the knowledge that she had done all she could to facilitate an open and welcoming environment. She reminded herself that honesty and vulnerability were at the heart of their connection, and that the coming conversation would only serve to deepen their understanding of one another.

Moments later, Mark and Amelia arrived, their presence filling the room with a mixture of anticipation and curiosity. Charlotte greeted them with a warm smile, her nerves momentarily forgotten in the presence of her two loves.

The three of them gathered around the table, the aroma of the carefully prepared meal filling the air. Charlotte's eyes darted between Mark and Amelia, observing their body language and searching for any sign of tension or discomfort.

As they settled into their seats, Charlotte's heart fluttered with a blend of excitement and apprehension. She took a moment to compose herself, knowing that the forthcoming conversation would shape the trajectory of their connections.

Amidst the clinking of glasses and the savoury flavours of the meal, the conversation unfolded. They discussed their thoughts, fears, and desires with a level of honesty that only deepened the bond between them. Charlotte's nervousness gradually dissolved as she witnessed the genuine interest and empathy that Mark and Amelia expressed for one another.

In the warmth of the living room, a sense of unity emerged. Mark and Amelia shared their perspectives and concerns, opening up to the possibilities that lay before them. Their shared willingness to listen and understand created an atmosphere of acceptance and mutual respect.

As the dessert was served, Charlotte couldn't help but feel a surge of joy and relief. Her longing for a harmonious connection between Mark and Amelia had been met with understanding and an eagerness to navigate the complexities of polyamory together.

In that moment, the nervousness that had accompanied Charlotte throughout the day melted away, replaced by a deep sense of gratitude. She knew that the journey ahead would not be without its challenges, but their shared commitment to honesty and open communication would guide them through.

As they enjoyed the sweetness of the cake and the laughter that filled the room, Charlotte couldn't help but revel in the knowledge that the first meeting between Mark and Amelia had laid the foundation for a future filled with growth, love, and the exploration of their unique connections.

The atmosphere in the room grew hushed as Mark broached the subject, his curiosity evident in his eyes. Amelia's expression turned serious, a hint of vulnerability shining through as she prepared to share a deeply personal part of her life.

Amelia took a deep breath, her voice steady yet filled with emotion, as she began to share her truth.

Amelia: "Mark, there's something I need to share with you, something that has shaped my perspective on starting a family. I experienced a difficult time in my past, as I was once forced to undergo an abortion against my will. It was a traumatic experience that left a lasting impact on me."

Mark's eyes widened with empathy, his understanding of the weight behind Amelia's words growing.

Mark: "Amelia, I'm so sorry to hear that you had to endure such a painful experience. I can't imagine what you went through."

Amelia nodded, appreciating Mark's compassion and willingness to listen.

Amelia: "Thank you, Mark. It has taken time and healing, but I have come to a point where I deeply desire to become a mother. I want to experience the joy and love that comes with raising a child, to create a nurturing environment and share my life with someone who is part of both of us."

Mark listened intently; his gaze unwavering as he absorbed Amelia's words. The weight of her desire to have a child resonated deeply with him.

Mark: "Amelia, your desire to become a mother is something I can understand. As I've reached the age of 35, I've also contemplated starting a family. I want to experience the joy of parenthood and share the love that comes with raising a child."

A sense of unity and understanding settled in the room, as both Amelia and Mark recognized the shared desire for parenthood. They exchanged a glance, a silent acknowledgment of the newfound alignment in their desires.

Amelia: "Mark, I understand if this is unexpected or if you need time to process. It's a significant decision, and I don't want you to feel pressured. But if we're both ready, I would like us to start trying for a child as soon as possible."

Mark smiled, his eyes shining with a mix of excitement and determination.

Mark: "Amelia, I don't need time to think about it. I'm ready. I've come to a point in my life where I feel the strong desire to become a father. If we're both aligned in this decision, let's embark on this journey together."

Amelia's face lit up with a mixture of relief and joy, knowing that they were on the same page. The prospect of creating a family brought a newfound sense of purpose and fulfilment to their connection.

The room was filled with an air of hope and anticipation, as their desires for a child merged with the love and commitment, they held for one another. They knew that the road ahead would have its challenges, but their shared determination and the strength of their connection would guide them through.

In that moment, the room seemed to radiate with the possibilities of a future that included love, parenthood, and the exploration of their polyamorous relationship. Their united desire for a child became a beacon of hope, illuminating the path they were about to embark upon together.

Tears welled up in Charlotte's eyes, a mixture of joy and overwhelming emotions flooding her being. Her heart swelled with love and gratitude for the connection she had with both Amelia and Mark. She took a moment to compose herself, her voice filled with a mixture of vulnerability and joy.

Charlotte: "I... I'm so incredibly happy. The idea of raising a child with both of you fills me with an indescribable sense of joy. To think that we can embark on this journey together, supporting and loving one another as we bring a new life into the world... It's truly a dream come true."

Amelia and Mark exchanged glances, their eyes shimmering with affection and a shared understanding. They reached out, each placing a hand on Charlotte's, their touch a comforting reassurance.

Amelia: "Charlotte, your happiness means the world to us. We want nothing more than to create a loving and supportive environment for our child, where they will be cherished by all three of us. Your willingness to be part of this journey fills our hearts with so much love and gratitude."

Mark nodded, his voice filled with sincerity and tenderness.

Mark: "Charlotte, you have brought so much love and fulfilment into our lives. The fact that you are willing to raise a child with us, to be a part of this incredible journey, fills me with a sense of profound gratitude. I can't wait to experience the joys of parenthood alongside both of you."

As their hands remained intertwined, a shared sense of unity and anticipation filled the room. The decision to embark on this journey of parenthood together had solidified their bond, strengthening the love and commitment they held for one another.

Charlotte wiped away her tears, a radiant smile gracing her lips.

Charlotte: "I am honoured and excited to be on this path with both of you. We have the opportunity to create a family rooted in love, trust, and open communication. I know that there will be challenges, but I believe that together we can navigate them with grace and unwavering support."

Amelia and Mark leaned in, wrapping Charlotte in a warm embrace. In that moment, they revealed in the joy of their shared decision, knowing that their love would extend to the precious life they were about to create. They understood that their journey as a polyamorous family would be unique, filled with its own joys and complexities.

With hearts aligned and their bond deepened, they embraced the future with a renewed sense of purpose and determination. They were ready to embark on the beautiful journey of parenthood together, cherishing every moment, and creating a loving and nurturing environment for their child.

As they held each other, their love formed an unbreakable bond—a bond that would guide them through the joys and challenges of raising a child together, and one that would forever shape their connection as a polyamorous family.

Amelia's voice carried a tone of concern and care as she broached the topic, recognizing the importance of ensuring a healthy environment for their future child. She turned to Charlotte and Mark, her eyes reflecting a mix of determination and love.

Amelia: "I think it's important for us to have a comprehensive understanding of our viral profiles before we start trying to conceive. It's a precautionary measure to ensure the safety and well-being of our child. What do you both think?"

Charlotte and Mark exchanged glances, their shared commitment to creating a safe and healthy environment evident in their expressions. They nodded in agreement, their voices filled with understanding and support.

Charlotte: "Amelia, I completely understand your concern, and I agree that it's a responsible step to take. We want to ensure that our child has the best possible start in life. Let's go ahead and schedule the blood tests."

Mark chimed in; his voice filled with conviction.

Mark: "I couldn't agree more. The well-being of our child is of utmost importance. By understanding our viral profiles, we can take any necessary precautions and make informed decisions to safeguard their health. Let's plan for the blood tests next week."

Amelia's eyes softened with gratitude, appreciating the unwavering support and understanding from both Charlotte and Mark.

Amelia: "Thank you both for being so understanding. This is a testament to the love and care we have for our future child. I'll take the initiative to schedule the appointments and ensure that everything is organized for next week."

As they made their plans, a sense of unity and shared responsibility settled within their hearts. They knew that this step was not only about their individual health but also about the collective well-being of their growing family.

Charlotte reached out, gently squeezing Amelia's hand, a gesture of reassurance and solidarity.

Charlotte: "Amelia, I'm grateful for your attention to detail and your commitment to the well-being of our child. Your love and care shine through in every decision we make. We are in this together, as a team."

Amelia smiled, her eyes shining with love and gratitude.

Amelia: "And I am grateful for both of you, for your understanding and support. We are embarking on this journey together, and I know that we will navigate any challenges that come our way with grace and strength. Our child will be surrounded by a foundation of love and protection."

In that moment, their bond grew even stronger. They were reminded of the depth of their love and the unwavering commitment they had made to one another and to the future they were building together.

As they continued to plan and prepare for their blood tests, the anticipation and excitement for their shared journey intensified. They were ready to embrace the responsibilities of parenthood with open hearts, open minds, and a steadfast dedication to creating a loving and healthy environment for their child.

Chapter 9 Planting Roots, Building a Home

• • • •

TWO MONTHS HAD PASSED since Amelia, Charlotte, and Mark made the decision to embark on their journey together, embracing polyamory and the prospect of parenthood. During this time, their connection had deepened, and their love had blossomed in beautiful and unexpected ways. As they continued to navigate the complexities of their relationship, they decided it was time to take the next step—a step that would solidify their commitment and provide a physical space where they could build a life together.

With their combined resources and the shared dream of creating a home by the sea, they embarked on the search for their perfect haven. After weeks of meticulous planning and countless viewings, they finally stumbled upon a magnificent house in the Hamptons, a sprawling beachside property that seemed to hold the promise of endless possibilities.

The house stood tall and majestic, its white exterior glistening under the golden rays of the sun. Nestled amidst lush greenery and overlooking the sparkling ocean, it was a sight to behold. The grand entrance beckoned them forward, promising a sanctuary where their love and connection could flourish.

Stepping inside, they were greeted by a spacious foyer that exuded elegance and warmth. The rooms branched out in different directions, each holding its own unique charm. The house boasted six rooms, providing ample space for their growing family and the potential to create individual havens that reflected their personalities.

Amelia, Charlotte, and Mark explored each room with a mix of excitement and anticipation. They imagined the memories they would create within these walls, the laughter that would echo through the hallways, and the love that would fill each corner of the house.

The master bedroom, with its panoramic view of the ocean, spoke to their hearts. Its grandeur and tranquillity made it the perfect retreat, a place where they could find solace and connection. The other rooms offered versatility, providing spaces that could be transformed into nurseries, home offices, or artistic sanctuaries.

As they moved through the house, their excitement grew, their visions intertwining as they shared their dreams and desires for each room. The dining room, bathed in natural light, seemed to call out for family gatherings and intimate dinner parties. The cosy living room, with its comfortable sofas and crackling fireplace, held the promise of evenings spent cuddled up, sharing stories and laughter.

In the kitchen, their eyes gleamed with excitement as they envisioned preparing meals together, the aromas of their favourite dishes wafting through the air. They could almost taste the warmth and love that would fill the space, as they shared culinary adventures and experimented with flavours.

As they reached the backyard, their breath caught at the sight of a sprawling deck that led to a private, sandy beach. The gentle crashing of the waves provided a soothing melody, a reminder of the beauty that surrounded them. The yard itself held endless possibilities, a canvas upon which they could create a haven of relaxation and play.

The decision to purchase the house was unanimous—a resounding affirmation of their commitment and belief in the future they were building together. With the necessary paperwork signed and the keys in their hands, they embarked on the journey of transforming the house into a home.

Weeks flew by in a whirlwind of activity, as the three of them poured their hearts into infusing the house with their love and personal touches. Each room became a reflection of their individuality and shared aspirations.

Amelia's artistic flair manifested in vibrant paintings and sculptures that adorned the walls, infusing the house with a sense of creativity and imagination. Charlotte's eye for design transformed the rooms into inviting spaces, balancing elegance and comfort. Mark's passion for woodworking brought custom-made furniture pieces that added warmth and character to each corner.

Together, they painted walls, arranged furniture, and carefully selected decor that spoke to their souls. They laughed, danced, and shared moments of exhaustion and exhilaration as they transformed the house into their shared haven by the sea.

As the final touches were put in place, a sense of pride and fulfilment washed over them. They stood hand in hand, surveying the home they had built together—a testament to their love, resilience, and unwavering commitment to one another.

Amelia, Charlotte, and Mark moved through the house with a renewed sense of purpose and gratitude. Each room held its own story, a chapter in the narrative of their love and their shared journey. Their home was a sanctuary, a place where they could be their authentic selves, a testament to the beautiful complexities of their polyamorous relationship.

As the sun began to set, casting a golden glow over their haven, they gathered on the deck, their faces filled with awe and contentment. With the sound of the ocean as their backdrop, they toasted to their new beginning, embracing the love and abundance that surrounded them.

Their home became a testament to the possibilities of love—a sanctuary where they could grow, evolve, and nurture their connection. Together, they embarked on the next chapter of their journey, grateful for the haven they had created—a place where their love would forever find solace and thrive, guided by the boundless depths of their hearts.

Chapter 10 The Tapestry of Love: Creating a Home Together

Amelia's bedroom serves as her haven—a sanctuary where she can immerse herself in tranquillity and express her artistic spirit. The walls are adorned with soft, pastel hues that create a serene and calming atmosphere, inviting a sense of peace and relaxation. The room is adorned with vibrant artwork, a testament to Amelia's creative prowess and passion. Each stroke of colour tells a story, reflecting her inner world and serving as a source of inspiration.

Near the window, a cosy reading nook beckons Amelia to unwind and lose herself in the pages of a book. The sunlight filters through the curtains, casting a gentle glow on the comfortable armchair and the stack of novels resting on a nearby table. It's a space where Amelia can escape into different worlds, allowing her imagination to roam freely.

The centrepiece of Amelia's haven is the bed, draped in flowing curtains that lend an air of ethereal beauty. Soft linens and plush pillows provide a cocoon of comfort, inviting her to sink into a peaceful slumber each night. With a delicate balance of elegance and cosiness, the bed becomes a sanctuary for rest and rejuvenation, a place where Amelia can find solace and inspiration after a long day.

Mark's bedroom, on the other hand, reflects his affinity for simplicity and functionality. The decor embodies a minimalist aesthetic, with clean lines and neutral tones dominating the space. The walls are adorned with carefully selected photographs and mementos from his travels, capturing moments of adventure and inspiration. Each image tells a story—a reminder of the places he's explored and the experiences that have shaped him.

A spacious desk occupies a corner of the room, bathed in natural light streaming through the window. It serves as a dedicated space for Mark to immerse himself in his work and creative pursuits. On its surface, a laptop and notebooks lay in perfect order, reflecting his dedication and passion. The desk becomes a hub of productivity, allowing Mark to channel his focus and energy into his projects and endeavours.

The bed in Mark's retreat is a haven of comfort, enveloping him in a sea of plush pillows and soft linens. It's a place where he can find respite and recharge his spirit, offering a peaceful sanctuary at the end of each day. The simplicity of the room allows for clarity of mind, providing a space where Mark can truly unwind and find solace in the serenity that surrounds him.

In Charlotte's oasis, her bedroom becomes a reflection of her personality and a testament to her love for literature and personal treasures. The walls are adorned with shelves that house her favourite books, each volume holding a story or an idea that has touched her soul. Treasured trinkets and cherished mementos occupy the remaining spaces, showcasing her love for collecting meaningful artifacts that hold sentimental value.

The warm, earthy tones of the room create an inviting ambiance, evoking a sense of cosiness and comfort. A vanity table, adorned with a well-lit mirror, becomes a space for Charlotte to indulge in moments of self-care and reflection. It's a place where she can nurture her inner world, finding inspiration and a sense of grounding.

At the heart of Charlotte's oasis lies the bed—a sanctuary of dreams and relaxation. Adorned with plush pillows and soft blankets, it becomes a place where she can retreat and recharge her spirit. The room exudes a sense of warmth and serenity, a reflection of Charlotte's desire for a tranquil haven within their shared home.

As they prepare for the arrival of their little ones, they create unique and nurturing spaces for their children. The baby girl's room is a haven of sweetness and tenderness, adorned with soft pink hues and delicate floral patterns. It is designed to embrace the nurturing spirit of a loving home.

The baby boy's room, on the other hand, is a vibrant space filled with energy and playfulness. Shades of blue adorn the walls, complemented by whimsical murals of animals and nature. It is a space where adventure and exploration are encouraged, fostering a sense of curiosity and wonder.

Finally, the conception chamber holds a sacred significance within their home. Adorned with luxurious fabrics and soft lighting, it becomes a haven of passion and intimacy—a space dedicated to the deep connection and desire between Amelia, Charlotte, and Mark. The bed, with its silky sheets and plush pillows, becomes a vessel for their love and longing, embracing their desires and dreams.

Each bedroom within their shared home tells a unique story—a reflection of the individuals who occupy them and the love that binds them together. From serenity and artistic flair to simplicity and functionality, their bedrooms are spaces where they can retreat, rejuvenate, and celebrate the beauty of their connection.

The long-awaited moment had finally arrived—the first night in their newly created home, a space that symbolized their love, commitment, and shared dreams. After two months of building a foundation and preparing their hearts, Amelia, Charlotte, and Mark found themselves on the cusp of a new chapter in their lives—the creation of their family.

As the evening unfolded, a palpable sense of anticipation filled the air. The house, now a sanctuary of their love, seemed to pulse with energy and possibility. The bedrooms, adorned with their personal touches, whispered promises of intimacy and connection. In their hearts, they knew that this night would hold profound significance—a convergence of desire, fertility, and the shared dream of bringing a child into the world.

Amidst this newfound anticipation, life's synchronicities seemed to unfold in mysterious ways. Both Charlotte and Amelia found themselves in the fertile phase of their cycles, an alignment that deepened their connection and fuelled their hopes of conceiving a child together. It was a serendipitous moment—one they acknowledged with gratitude and reverence.

As the evening wore on, the three of them gathered in the sacred space of the conception chamber. The room, adorned with luxurious fabrics and soft lighting, held an aura of intimacy and possibility. Their hearts were filled with a mixture of excitement, vulnerability, and profound love as they embarked on this intimate journey to parenthood.

Mark, ready to embrace this moment, led the way with a tenderness that mirrored his devotion. Together, they stepped into the chamber, the weight of their dreams and desires propelling them forward. In this sacred space, time seemed to stand still as they embraced the beauty of their connection and the boundless potential for new life.

With hearts intertwined and a deep understanding of their desires, they embarked on an intimate dance—a dance that celebrated their love, trust, and shared commitment to building a family. In this chamber of creation, their bodies merged, their desires melded, and their spirits soared. They surrendered to the depths of passion, vulnerability, and the profound connection that bound them together.

Amidst the whispers of love and the echoes of their shared dreams, they revealed in the power of this moment. Each touch, each caress, and each breath carried a weight of purpose—a purpose that went beyond their individual desires and expanded into the realm of creating a life, a future, and a legacy of love.

As the night unfolded, their bodies danced in harmony—a symphony of desire, pleasure, and vulnerability. Time seemed to lose its hold as they embraced the magic of this shared experience, their hearts beating in unison. In this sacred union, they merged not only their physical bodies but also their hopes, dreams, and intentions for the life they yearned to bring into existence.

As the night slowly gave way to dawn, their bodies entwined and their souls intertwined, they lay together in the afterglow. In the silence, their breaths mingled, a gentle reminder of the profound connection they had forged. Their hearts overflowed with gratitude—for this moment, for their love, and for the infinite possibilities that lay before them.

The first night in their newly created home had become a tapestry of love—a testament to their commitment, vulnerability, and shared vision of building a family. As they drifted into sleep, their dreams were filled with the whispers of a future filled with love, laughter, and the pitter-patter of tiny feet. Together, they had embarked on a journey that would forever transform their lives, their love, and the legacy they would create as a polyamorous family.

Chapter 11 A new business is born

• • • •

THREE MONTHS HAD PASSED since Charlotte, Amelia, and Mark had found their rhythm as a polyamorous family, embracing a love that defied societal norms and traditional expectations. During this time, their bond had deepened, their connections had grown stronger, and their lives had become a tapestry of passion, intimacy, and emotional fulfilment.

As the days turned into weeks, Charlotte found herself pondering the path they had taken. The journey of self-discovery and exploration had not only transformed their lives but had also ignited a spark within her—an idea that flickered with the potential to impact others who sought love beyond the boundaries of monogamy.

One evening, as the three of them sat together, basking in the warmth of their shared love, Charlotte tentatively broached the subject that had been occupying her thoughts. Her voice trembled with a mix of excitement and vulnerability as she revealed her idea—to write a book about their experiences, their journey into polyamory, and the lessons they had learned along the way.

Amelia's eyes sparkled with curiosity and support, while Mark's gaze held a mixture of intrigue and encouragement. They listened attentively as Charlotte shared her vision—a book that would shed light on the beauty and complexities of polyamory, offering guidance and inspiration to those who dared to venture beyond the confines of societal expectations.

As the discussion deepened, their shared enthusiasm grew. They realized that their journey had not only transformed their own lives but also held the potential to help others navigate the uncharted waters of polyamory. They saw an opportunity to share their experiences, challenges, and triumphs, providing a roadmap for those seeking a similar path to love and fulfilment.

With their collective wisdom and unique perspectives, they brainstormed ideas for the book—chapters on communication, jealousy, navigating multiple relationships, and building a strong foundation of trust and understanding. They envisioned a book that would not only educate but also inspire, offering a beacon of hope for individuals who felt trapped within the confines of monogamy but yearned for a more expansive and authentic expression of love.

As the excitement filled the room, they made a pact—to embark on this literary journey together. Charlotte would be the writer, weaving their stories and insights into a tapestry of words. Amelia and Mark would offer their perspectives, sharing their own experiences and providing invaluable insights that would enrich the book.

Days turned into weeks, and Charlotte immersed herself in the process of writing. She poured her heart and soul onto the pages, capturing the essence of their polyamorous journey—the joy, the challenges, the vulnerability, and the profound sense of connection that had blossomed among them.

Throughout the writing process, Charlotte found herself reflecting on their experiences—the incredible sexual and emotional encounters, the depths of their love, and the uncharted territories they had navigated as a polyamorous triad. She marvelled at the depth of their connection, the growth they had experienced individually and as a family, and the unwavering support they had provided one another.

As the manuscript took shape, Charlotte realized that their story was not just about their own personal journey, but a testament to the resilience and courage of all those who dared to embrace polyamory. She hoped that their words would serve as a guiding light for individuals who longed for love that transcended societal norms, helping them navigate the complexities and challenges that accompanied this unconventional path.

Simultaneously, Charlotte's entrepreneurial spirit stirred within her. Inspired by their own journey, she recognized an opportunity to create a dating agency—a space where individuals seeking polyamorous connections could find support, guidance, and potential partners who embraced the same values and desires.

With Mark's business acumen and Amelia's support, they embarked on this new venture together. They established the foundations of the agency, envisioning a safe and inclusive space that would facilitate connections and foster a community of like-minded individuals seeking love, connection, and fulfilment in non-traditional relationships.

As the book neared completion and the dating agency took shape, Charlotte's heart swelled with a sense of purpose and fulfilment. She recognized the transformative power of their journey and the potential to inspire and support others in finding their own paths to love and fulfilment.

The day arrived when Charlotte typed the final words of their book—a testament to their love, their commitment, and the beauty of polyamory. With Amelia and Mark by her side, they celebrated this milestone—a tangible representation of their journey and their desire to share their experiences with the world.

As they closed the chapter on their book, they embraced the next chapter of their lives—the launch of the dating agency. They held hands, their hearts filled with hope and excitement, as they embarked on this new endeavour, extending their reach and creating a space where others could find the love and connection they had discovered.

Together, they had not only transformed their own lives but had also ignited a spark that would guide and inspire others on their own journeys of love, authenticity, and fulfilment. As they looked toward the future, they knew that their legacy would go beyond their own love story, leaving an indelible mark on the hearts of those who dared to redefine love on their own terms.

With a sense of purpose and determination, Charlotte embarked on the journey of writing their polyamory book. As the words flowed from her fingertips, she poured her heart and soul into the manuscript. The experiences, the challenges, and the transformative moments they had shared as a polyamorous family became the essence of the book—a testament to their love and a guide for others seeking a similar path.

However, Charlotte made a decision that would shape the course of her journey as an author. She chose to write the book under a pseudonym, keeping her identity anonymous. This choice allowed her to share their story with honesty and vulnerability while protecting their privacy. It was a conscious decision, rooted in the belief that the message and lessons of the book should take precedence over personal recognition.

As Charlotte delved deeper into the writing process, she found solace in anonymity. The words flowed freely, unburdened by the weight of public scrutiny. She felt liberated to explore the depths of their polyamorous journey, unencumbered by the fear of judgment or prejudice. This pseudonym became her shield, allowing her to fully embrace her role as a storyteller without the constraints of personal exposure.

As the manuscript neared completion, Charlotte faced a critical decision—how to publish the book and share it with the world. She wanted to ensure that their message reached as many people as possible, to offer support, guidance, and inspiration to those who longed for love beyond traditional boundaries. After much contemplation, she chose to submit the manuscript to a publishing company without disclosing her true identity.

Unbeknownst to her, the publishing company was owned by her father—a successful businessman who had made a name for himself in the literary world. The manuscript resonated deeply with him, evoking emotions he couldn't quite explain. Recognizing the potential impact of the book, he made the decision to publish it, unaware that his own daughter was the brilliant mind behind the words.

As the book hit the shelves, its impact reverberated throughout the literary world. The pseudonymous author gained attention and acclaim for the rawness and authenticity of the storytelling. Readers were captivated by the intimate portrayal of polyamory—a topic that had long been stigmatized and misunderstood. The book became a beacon of hope and validation for those who yearned for a love that defied societal norms.

Sales skyrocketed as readers embraced the message of the book, finding solace, validation, and guidance within its pages. The pseudonymous author became a mystery, a symbol of liberation and possibility, captivating the literary world with her anonymity and the power of her words.

Meanwhile, Charlotte silently watched the success of her book from the side-lines. Her heart swelled with pride and gratitude as she witnessed the impact it had on readers' lives. The decision to remain anonymous had allowed her to separate herself from the book's reception and focus solely on the message it conveyed. She found solace in knowing that their story was making a difference, even if her identity remained hidden.

The success of the book opened doors for their dating agency business. As readers resonated with their story and sought to explore their own journeys of non-traditional love, the agency became a platform for like-minded individuals to connect and forge meaningful relationships. The business thrived, offering a safe and inclusive space where individuals could explore polyamory and discover the love and connection they craved.

Within the literary world, the pseudonymous author became a sensation—a voice that defied expectations and challenged societal norms. Critics praised the book's insights, raw emotion, and the anonymous author's ability to capture the complexities and beauty of polyamory. Interviews and discussions centred around the mysterious writer, igniting debates about the importance of anonymity and the power of storytelling.

Meanwhile, Charlotte continued to navigate the delicate balance of anonymity and public recognition. She watched as her book resonated with countless readers, validating their own experiences and inspiring them to embrace their authentic desires. It was a bittersweet feeling, knowing that her personal journey had touched the lives of so many, yet remaining hidden behind a pseudonym.

In the depths of her heart, Charlotte found solace in the impact she was making, even if her true identity remained concealed. She understood that the power of the book was not in the name behind the words, but in the message itself—a message that transcended individual identities and spoke to the universal longing for love, connection, and fulfilment.

As the book continued to thrive and the dating agency flourished, Charlotte embraced her role as a catalyst for change. She saw the impact of their story and the power of vulnerability and honesty. And while her anonymity protected her personal life, it did not diminish the profound sense of purpose and fulfilment she felt in her heart.

In the end, it wasn't the recognition or personal accolades that drove Charlotte—it was the knowledge that their story had touched lives, opened minds, and offered hope to those who dared to redefine love on their own terms. She had found her purpose in sharing their journey, in guiding others toward the love and fulfilment they deserved. And in the depths of her anonymity, Charlotte found a profound sense of fulfilment—an affirmation that sometimes, the truest impact is made when the individual takes a step back, allowing the message to shine brightly on its own.

Chapter 12 A Journey of Acceptance and Understanding

Later, she took the decision to tell the truth to her father. She met him.

Charlotte: Dad, can we talk?

Father: Of course, Charlotte. What's on your mind?

Charlotte: I want to tell you something important, something that I've been keeping from you for a while now. It's about the book that you published.

Father: Oh, yes! It's been quite a success, hasn't it? I'm proud of the impact it's had.

Charlotte: Thank you, Dad. I'm glad you feel that way, but there's something you should know. I am the author of that book.

Father: (Surprised) You? But... I had no idea. Why did you keep it a secret?

Charlotte: I chose to write under a pseudonym because I wanted the book to be about the message, not about the person behind it. I wanted it to resonate with readers on its own merits, without any personal bias or attention on me.

Father: I understand your intention, Charlotte, but I must admit I feel a mix of emotions right now. Surprise, yes, but also pride that my own daughter has written such a powerful and impactful book.

Charlotte: Thank you, Dad. I'm grateful for your understanding. It wasn't an easy decision to keep it a secret, but I believed it was necessary for the book to reach its full potential.

Father: I respect your choice, Charlotte, and I'm proud of you for the courage and talent you've shown in writing this book. I can see now why it resonated with so many readers. But I have to admit, I have some concerns too.

Charlotte: I understand, Dad. What are your concerns?

Father: Well, this book tells a very personal and unconventional story about your polyamorous family. I can't help but worry about how it might affect our family's reputation and your own personal life.

Charlotte: Dad, I've thought about that too, and I want you to know that I've taken precautions to protect our privacy and the privacy of Amelia and Mark. The decision to write anonymously was made with their consent and in consideration of their own desires for privacy. I would never do anything to intentionally harm our family.

Father: I appreciate your consideration, Charlotte, and your reassurance eases some of my concerns. But I have to admit, I need time to process this information and understand how it fits into our lives.

Charlotte: I understand, Dad, and I respect your need for time. But I want you to know that this book was not written to defy or challenge our family. It was written to share a story of love, acceptance, and the pursuit of happiness beyond societal norms. I hope that, with time, you can come to see the beauty in our family's journey.

Father: It will take time, Charlotte, but I love you, and I will always strive to accept and support you. Your happiness and fulfilment are important to me, and I trust that the choices you've made are grounded in your own truth. We will find a way to navigate this new chapter together.

Charlotte: Thank you, Dad. Your love and acceptance mean the world to me. I believe that, in time, you will come to understand and accept our family just as you have accepted the choices and differences of others. We are still your family, and our love for each other is unwavering.

Father: You're right, Charlotte. Love should always triumph over judgment and societal expectations. I may not fully comprehend your journey, but I will do my best to be there for you and support you as your father.

Charlotte: That's all I can ask for, Dad. Thank you for listening and for your willingness to try to understand. Our family may be unconventional, but it's rooted in love, respect, and a shared desire for happiness. Together, we can overcome any challenges that come our way.

In that heartfelt conversation, Charlotte and her father embarked on a new chapter of understanding and acceptance. It was a turning point—a moment that marked the beginning of their continued growth as a family. In their shared commitment to love and support, they found strength and resilience, paving the way for a future where love knew no bounds and acceptance knew no limitations.

In a quiet moment, after Charlotte had shared her truth with her father, her mother entered the room. There was a sense of anticipation, as Charlotte wondered how her mother would respond to the revelation. With a mixture of nervousness and hope, she began to explain what she had told her father.

Charlotte: Mom, I need to talk to you. I just had a conversation with Dad, and I revealed something important to him.

Mother: (Curious) What is it, Charlotte? You seem a bit anxious.

Charlotte: I told Dad about the book I wrote and the fact that I am the pseudonymous author. I shared our story, our journey into polyamory, and the impact it has had on our lives.

Mother: (Surprised) Oh my, Charlotte! That is quite a revelation. I had no idea. How did your father react?

Charlotte: He needed some time to process the information, but ultimately, he accepted it and expressed his love and support. It was a mix of emotions for both of us, but he reassured me that he would strive to understand and accept our family as it is.

Mother: (Pensive) I see. That must have been a lot to take in for him. And how do you feel about his response?

Charlotte: Mom, I'm relieved and grateful that he's willing to try to understand. It means a lot to me. We had a heartfelt conversation, and although there may be challenges along the way, his acceptance gives me hope.

Mother: (Thoughtful) That's wonderful, Charlotte. I'm glad your father has chosen to support you. But what about me? How do you think I'll react?

Charlotte: Mom, I hope that you can find it in your heart to accept our family as well. I know our journey is unconventional, but our love for each other remains steadfast. I wanted to share our story not to challenge or upset you, but to help others who may be on a similar path and searching for acceptance and understanding.

Mother: (Embracing Charlotte) My dear Charlotte, I love you more than words can express. I may not fully understand or have anticipated this journey, but your happiness and fulfilment are of utmost importance to me. I will do my best to embrace our family as it is and support you every step of the way.

In that tender moment, mother and daughter found solace in each other's arms. Their love transcended the complexities of their family's unconventional journey, grounding them in a shared commitment to acceptance and understanding. It was a testament to the unbreakable bond between a mother and her child—a bond that could weather any storm and embrace the uniqueness of their family's love.

As the days turned into weeks and the weeks into months, Charlotte's family navigated the intricacies of their new normal. They faced challenges and uncertainties, but their love and support for one another remained unwavering. With each passing day, the strength of their family unit grew, fuelled by the acceptance, understanding, and open-heartedness that they had embraced.

Their journey became a testament to the power of unconditional love—a love that could transcend societal expectations and embrace the uniqueness of each individual's path. It was a love that celebrated the beauty in diversity, recognizing that love and acceptance had no boundaries.

As Charlotte, her mother, and her father embarked on this new chapter together, they forged a deeper connection—a connection grounded in authenticity, vulnerability, and a shared commitment to love unconditionally. Their family became a testament to the resilience of the human spirit, the power of acceptance, and the transformative nature of love.

In the tapestry of their lives, they weaved a story of love, acceptance, and growth—a story that inspired others to embrace their own unique journeys and find solace in the arms of those who truly loved and understood them. And in the end, it was the love and acceptance within their family that became their greatest strength—a force that would guide them through any challenges that lay ahead.

As the days turned into weeks, Charlotte's parents grew more curious about the life she had created with Amelia and Mark. They had come to accept and support their daughter's polyamorous journey, and now, they wanted to embrace it fully. With open hearts and a sense of adventure, they made plans to visit Charlotte's secret home and meet Amelia and Mark for the first time.

The day arrived, and excitement filled the air as Charlotte's parents stepped into the home that had become a haven of love and acceptance. The warm embrace between Charlotte and her parents reflected the deep connection they shared, now strengthened by their mutual understanding and support.

Amelia and Mark welcomed Charlotte's parents with open arms, their smiles radiating warmth and hospitality. The initial hesitations that often accompany such encounters melted away as they exchanged stories, laughter, and shared experiences. It was as if they had known each other for years, united by a common love for Charlotte and a desire to create a harmonious family unit.

As the sun set, the aroma of a sizzling barbecue filled the air, drawing everyone to the outdoor patio. Charlotte's father, eager to experience this unique family dynamic, joined Mark in grilling the mouth-watering delicacies. The sound of laughter and conversation filled the air as they savoured the delicious flavours and shared stories from their own lives.

The father, intrigued by the ambiance and the vibrant energy of the home, couldn't help but notice a door marked with the initials "CC." His curiosity piqued; he couldn't resist asking about its significance.

Father: (With a hint of curiosity) Charlotte, may I ask about the room with the initials "CC"? I noticed it earlier, and my curiosity got the best of me.

Charlotte: (Smiling) Oh, Dad, that's the Conception Chamber. It's a special room for intimate moments and the conception of our family's future. We wanted to create a space that symbolized our hopes and dreams.

Father: (Surprised, his face turning slightly red) Ah, I see. Well, I must admit, that caught me off guard. It's certainly a unique touch to your home.

Charlotte: (Gently) I understand, Dad. It may seem unconventional, but it's a representation of the love and commitment we have to each other and our shared journey. It's a room filled with hope and the desire to create a family filled with love and joy.

The father, although momentarily taken aback, recognized the depth of love and intention behind their unique home. He realized that this room, with its initials emblazoned on the door, was a testament to his daughter's unwavering determination to create a family built on love and acceptance.

As the evening progressed, the conversation flowed effortlessly, weaving a tapestry of shared experiences, dreams, and aspirations. They indulged in a delightful dessert of French cheeses, accompanied by a rich Bordeaux wine—a nod to the blending of cultures and traditions that had brought them together.

In that moment, gathered around the table, Charlotte's parents marvelled at the love and connection they witnessed within this unconventional family. They were filled with a profound sense of gratitude for the journey that had led them to this moment of unity, acceptance, and understanding.

The evening ended with hugs, laughter, and promises to stay connected and nurture the bonds that had formed. As Charlotte's parents bid their farewell, they carried with them a newfound appreciation for the beauty of diversity, the strength of love, and the power of acceptance.

From that day forward, Charlotte's parents became an integral part of her polyamorous family. Their love and support transcended societal expectations, embracing the limitless possibilities that love could bring. Together, they embarked on a shared journey—one that would forever deepen their connection, celebrate their differences, and strengthen the unbreakable bond of family.

In the hearts of Charlotte, Amelia, Mark, and her parents, a new chapter had begun—one filled with love, acceptance, and the harmonious blending of lives and hearts. Their shared experiences would continue to shape their story, reminding them of the transformative power of love, understanding, and the joy that comes from embracing the unconventional with open arms.

Chapter 13 Multiple pregnancies

One year later the two women were pregnant of Mark.

Amelia's pregnancy was a time of anticipation, joy, and deep connection. As her belly grew, she radiated a maternal glow, embracing the miracle of life growing within her. Throughout the months, Mark and Charlotte stood by her side, offering unwavering support and showering her with love and care.

Together, they embarked on a journey of preparation, attending prenatal appointments, reading books, and creating a nurturing environment for their unborn child. Amelia's pregnancy was filled with moments of awe and wonder, as they felt the baby's movements and listened to the rhythmic sound of their little one's heartbeat.

As July arrived, Amelia went into labour, surrounded by the love and presence of her chosen family. The room was filled with a sense of excitement and anticipation as they awaited the arrival of their precious boy, Nate. The atmosphere was one of serenity and support, with soothing music playing softly in the background.

Amelia's strength and determination shone through as she brought Nate into the world, guided by the supportive hands of both Mark and Charlotte. Their combined presence and love provided her with the courage to endure the challenges of childbirth. The room was filled with tears of joy and overwhelming emotion as Nate took his first breath and nestled into his mother's loving arms.

Just a couple of months later, it was Charlotte's turn to experience the miracle of pregnancy. Her journey was filled with a sense of awe and wonder, as her body transformed to nurture the life growing within her. Amelia and Mark showered her with love and support, cherishing each milestone of this extraordinary time.

As the months passed, Charlotte felt the gentle kicks and flutters of her baby girl, Rose, a beautiful reminder of the life that blossomed within her. Together with Amelia and Mark, they prepared for Rose's arrival, attending birthing classes and creating a nurturing space for their daughter.

In September, the air was filled with anticipation as Charlotte went into labour. Surrounded by the love and support of her chosen family, she embraced the power of her body and the profound journey of bringing new life into the world. The room was filled with soft lighting, soothing scents, and the melodic sounds of nature, creating an atmosphere of tranquillity.

With Mark and Amelia by her side, Charlotte tapped into her inner strength and brought forth their daughter, Rose. It was a moment of pure magic, as their little girl entered the world, greeted by tears of joy and the warm embrace of her loving parents. Their hearts swelled with an overwhelming love and a deep sense of gratitude for this precious gift of life.

As the days turned into weeks and weeks into months, Nate and Rose grew, nurtured by the love and devotion of their parents, Amelia, Charlotte, and Mark. Their home was filled with laughter, coos, and the sweet melodies of lullabies. Together, they created a harmonious and loving environment, fostering a strong sense of family and connection.

Amelia, Charlotte, and Mark celebrated the milestones of their children with pride and joy, cherishing the unique bond they had as a polyamorous family. Each pregnancy and birth served as a reminder of the incredible power of love, acceptance, and the capacity of the human heart to expand and encompass the beauty of unconventional family dynamics.

Nate and Rose would grow up surrounded by a support system that embraced their individuality, celebrated their uniqueness, and nurtured their dreams. As they embarked on their own journeys, they would be guided by the love and wisdom of their parents and the unwavering connection of their extraordinary family.

In the embrace of their loving home, Amelia, Charlotte, Mark, Nate, and Rose would continue to navigate the beautiful complexities of life, cherishing the bond they shared and celebrating the extraordinary love that had brought them together.

As Amelia, Charlotte, and Mark welcomed Nate and Rose into their lives, their unwavering commitment to providing the best care for their children became their top priority. Together, they formed a united front, ensuring that their babies received the love, attention, and support they needed, especially during the nights when restful sleep was essential for both the little ones and their parents.

During the nights, they established a shared routine, where they would take turns attending to the needs of Nate and Rose. They recognized the importance of restful sleep for each other, knowing that well-rested parents would be better equipped to provide the utmost care for their children.

Amelia, Charlotte, and Mark created a nurturing environment in their home, ensuring that each baby had their own comfortable and safe sleeping space. They decorated the nursery rooms with soft colours, soothing melodies, and gentle lighting to create a peaceful atmosphere conducive to sleep.

In the early days and months, Amelia breastfed both Nate and Rose, providing them with the nourishment and connection that only a mother could offer. They embraced the concept of shared breastfeeding, where each baby had the opportunity to bond with Amelia during their feeding sessions. This approach allowed them to share the intimate experience of breastfeeding, deepening their connection as a family.

As the babies grew older, they introduced bottle feeding, allowing both Amelia and Mark to participate in the feeding process and share in the joy of nourishing their children. They carefully coordinated their schedules, ensuring that each baby was fed, burped, and comforted, providing the reassurance and warmth they needed during the night.

During those long nights, Amelia, Charlotte, and Mark relied on open communication and support to navigate the challenges that came with caring for two infants. They would often gather in the living room or kitchen, sharing stories, tips, and techniques to soothe and calm their babies.

When one baby needed attention, the other two would step in to lend a helping hand. They understood the importance of being present and responsive to the needs of their children, providing comfort, cuddles, and soothing words to help them feel secure and loved.

Throughout the night, they embraced the art of co-sleeping, creating a sense of closeness and connection. With their beds positioned in close proximity, they were able to respond quickly to their babies' needs, whether it be a feeding, a diaper change, or a comforting touch.

They also embraced the power of babywearing, using slings and carriers to keep their babies close during the night and throughout the day. This practice allowed them to provide physical closeness and warmth while attending to other tasks or simply enjoying quiet moments together as a family.

In the quiet hours of the night, as they cradled their babies in their arms, they would share stories, sing lullabies, and whisper words of love and affection. Their presence and touch provided a sense of security, allowing Nate and Rose to drift off into peaceful slumber.

As the nights turned into days and the days into weeks, their efforts to provide the best care for their children blossomed into a symphony of love, dedication, and unity. They embraced the challenges and joys that came with raising two infants, knowing that their unwavering commitment to each other and their little ones would guide them through every step of their parenting journey.

Amelia, Charlotte, and Mark stood as pillars of strength for their children, supporting one another in times of fatigue and uncertainty. Their nights were filled with tender moments, gentle touches, and the unwavering belief that their love, shared amongst the three of them, would create a nurturing and loving environment for Nate and Rose to thrive.

In the quiet embrace of the night, Amelia, Charlotte, and Mark found solace and joy in their shared role as parents, cherishing the unique connection they had as a polyamorous family. With love as their guide, they embraced the challenges and blessings of parenting, knowing that their united efforts would provide Nate and Rose with the best care in the world, both day and night.

Chapter 14 A new notoriety

L ife had been a beautiful whirlwind for Charlotte, Amelia, Mark, and their little ones, Nate and Rose. Their polyamorous family had thrived, and their dating agency business had blossomed beyond their wildest dreams. Each day brought new joys and challenges, but their love and commitment to each other carried them through.

On the occasion of Nate and Rose's second birthday, as they celebrated with friends and loved ones, an unexpected opportunity arose. A television channel had taken notice of Charlotte's book and their unique family dynamic. Intrigued by their story, they extended an invitation for Charlotte to share their journey in an interview.

Charlotte, feeling a mix of excitement and nervousness, pondered the invitation. She realized that this could be an opportunity to shed light on polyamory, to challenge societal norms, and to promote acceptance and understanding. With the support of Amelia and Mark, she decided to accept the interview, believing that their story could inspire and encourage others on similar paths.

The day of the interview arrived, and Charlotte, dressed in an outfit that reflected her confidence and authenticity, found herself sitting across from the interviewer. Cameras and lights filled the room, creating an atmosphere charged with anticipation.

Interviewer: "Charlotte, thank you for joining us today. Your book has captivated readers, and your family's unique journey has sparked intrigue. Can you share with us how your polyamorous relationship has influenced your life?"

Charlotte: "Thank you for having me. Our polyamorous relationship has been a beautiful and transformative journey. It has taught us the importance of open communication, honesty, and unconditional love. Our love for each other goes beyond societal norms, and it has allowed us to create a strong and nurturing environment for our children."

The interview continued as Charlotte eloquently shared their story, delving into the challenges they faced and the joys they experienced as a polyamorous family. She spoke of the power of love and acceptance, the strength of their bond, and the happiness they found in embracing their unconventional path.

Interviewer: "Charlotte, your story is inspiring. What message would you like to convey to others who may be navigating non-traditional relationships or struggling with societal expectations?"

Charlotte: "To those on similar paths, I want to say that love knows no boundaries. It is not confined by societal expectations or labels. Embrace your truth, be courageous in expressing your love, and surround yourself with those who support and uplift you. Remember, it is the power of love that creates families, and there is beauty in every unique journey."

The interview concluded, leaving an air of reflection and possibility. Charlotte's words, imbued with authenticity and vulnerability, resonated with viewers who yearned for acceptance and understanding in their own lives.

In the days following the interview, messages poured in from individuals and families who had found solace and hope in Charlotte's story. Her words had touched hearts, sparked conversations, and ignited a sense of empowerment within those who dared to embrace their own unconventional paths to love and happiness.

Charlotte, Amelia, Mark, Nate, and Rose continued to navigate their extraordinary journey with grace and resilience. They remained committed to their family, their business, and their mission to promote love, acceptance, and understanding in a world that often struggled to comprehend the beauty of diversity.

Their story, shared on the television screen, had become a catalyst for change—an invitation for society to question preconceived notions, to embrace the vastness of love, and to celebrate the resilience of the human spirit. In the face of adversity, they stood tall, united in their love and determination to make a positive impact on the world.

As Charlotte reflected on the unexpected turn her life had taken, she realized that their journey was far from over. They would continue to challenge societal norms, advocate for love in all its forms, and inspire others to live authentically and fearlessly.

Through the power of their story, their voices became a beacon of hope—a reminder that love, acceptance, and the courage to be true to oneself could transcend societal expectations and create a world where all forms of love were celebrated and embraced.

Their journey was a testament to the resilience of the human spirit and the transformative power of love—a reminder that, in the end, it was the power of love that would change the world, one heart at a time.

As Charlotte's story gained visibility through the television interview, it also caught the attention of social media platforms. People from all walks of life flocked to express their opinions, share their own experiences, and engage in discussions surrounding her polyamorous lifestyle and family dynamic. While many individuals resonated with her message of love, acceptance, and embracing non-traditional relationships, others harboured more aggressive and confrontational views.

Social media became a space of both support and hostility. As Charlotte shared her journey and advocated for love beyond societal norms, she encountered an array of reactions. Positive comments poured in from individuals who found inspiration in her story, expressing gratitude for the representation and the courage to live authentically.

Supportive comments filled the comment sections, with people expressing their admiration for Charlotte's bravery in sharing her experiences and challenging societal expectations. They applauded her for promoting acceptance, love, and understanding in a world that often clung to rigid norms.

However, amidst the positivity, Charlotte also faced a barrage of negative and aggressive comments from individuals who held opposing beliefs or were unable to comprehend her choices. These individuals resorted to personal attacks, judgment, and intolerance, revealing the deeply ingrained biases and prejudices that exist within society.

Charlotte, Amelia, Mark, and their extended family were no strangers to adversity. They had faced their fair share of challenges, and now, they found themselves navigating the often unpredictable and volatile landscape of social media. Although hurtful comments had the potential to affect them, they remained steadfast in their commitment to love, acceptance, and educating others about the beauty of diverse relationships.

Charlotte understood that not everyone would agree with her choices or embrace the concept of polyamory. However, she remained determined to use her platform to promote understanding and challenge societal norms that restricted the expression of love and happiness.

She engaged with the comments, responding to those who genuinely sought understanding, providing insights into her personal experiences, and engaging in meaningful dialogue. She hoped that by sharing her story with authenticity and vulnerability, she could foster empathy, open minds, and encourage a more compassionate society.

Additionally, Charlotte's supporters rallied around her, offering words of encouragement and standing up against the hostility. They provided a shield of positivity, creating a safe space within the online realm, where love, acceptance, and respectful dialogue flourished.

Charlotte's experiences on social media, though challenging, served as a reminder of the importance of continuing to advocate for love and acceptance in all its forms. It reaffirmed her commitment to fostering understanding, even in the face of adversity.

She remained resolute in her belief that change could be sparked through open conversations, education, and the promotion of empathy. She saw social media as both a powerful tool for spreading awareness and a platform for building bridges between different perspectives.

In the midst of the polarized reactions, Charlotte held on to the unwavering support of her loved ones and the knowledge that her message was reaching those who needed it most. She found solace in the outpouring of love and encouragement from individuals who resonated with her story and had also experienced judgment or discrimination due to their unconventional relationships.

Ultimately, Charlotte chose to focus on the positive impact she could make, remaining true to herself and her mission of promoting love, acceptance, and understanding. Through the noise and occasional hostility, she persevered, knowing that change begins with the courage to share one's truth and advocate for a more inclusive and compassionate world.

After the success of her first book and the overwhelming support she received, Charlotte found herself at a crossroads. The power of her words had sparked a fire within her, fuelling a desire to advocate for change on a larger scale. Inspired by her own experiences and driven by her unwavering commitment to love, acceptance, and equality, she made the bold decision to enter the race for the U.S. House of Representatives.

Charlotte believed that it was time to challenge the status quo and push for legislative reforms that recognized the validity of non-traditional relationships, including the right to enter into a marriage between three individuals. With the support of her loved ones, including Amelia and Mark, she embarked on a political journey fuelled by passion, determination, and the unwavering belief in the power of love to transcend boundaries.

Her decision to run as an independent candidate, free from the constraints of traditional party affiliations, was a testament to her commitment to be a voice for the marginalized, the underrepresented, and those seeking alternative paths to love and happiness.

As news of her candidacy spread, her second book, advocating for the recognition of three-person marriages, quickly became a bestseller. The public, captivated by her message of inclusivity and equality, rallied behind her, igniting a wave of support that transcended traditional political boundaries.

People from all walks of life were drawn to Charlotte's campaign, inspired by her authenticity, passion, and unwavering dedication to the values she championed. Supporters flooded her social media platforms, attended her campaign rallies, and generously contributed to her grassroots fundraising efforts.

Charlotte's platform called for legislative reform that would recognize and protect the rights of individuals in polyamorous relationships, advocating for equal legal recognition, benefits, and protections for all forms of consensual adult partnerships. Her message resonated with a growing segment of the population, challenging the traditional notions of love, family, and marriage.

As the election campaign unfolded, Charlotte embarked on a whirlwind of speeches, debates, and community engagements. She used these opportunities to educate the public, to challenge preconceived notions, and to build bridges of understanding. She presented her ideas with eloquence and conviction, sharing personal stories and experiences that humanized the polyamorous community and shed light on the need for comprehensive legal reforms.

The journey was not without its challenges. Charlotte faced opposition from those resistant to change, individuals bound by conservative ideals and deeply ingrained beliefs about what constituted a "traditional" family. However, she remained steadfast in her conviction that love knows no boundaries and that everyone deserves the same rights and opportunities to pursue happiness.

Charlotte's campaign became a movement, a call for the recognition and acceptance of diverse relationship structures. Her supporters, affectionately known as "Charlotte's Champions," became the face of a growing societal shift toward embracing non-traditional relationships and challenging outdated norms.

As Election Day approached, the excitement and anticipation reached its peak. The outcome of the race would not only determine Charlotte's political future but also serve as a barometer for the progress of societal acceptance and equality.

On that fateful day, as the votes were tallied, Charlotte's journey reached a pivotal moment. She emerged victorious, having secured a seat in the U.S. House of Representatives. Her victory was a triumph for love, equality, and the power of authentic representation.

In the halls of Congress, Charlotte became a tireless advocate for the rights of individuals in non-traditional relationships, using her platform to champion legislative reforms that recognized the validity and importance of all forms of love and family.

Her presence in the political landscape sent ripples of change throughout the nation, igniting conversations, challenging prejudices, and inspiring others to stand up for their own truths. She became a beacon of hope for marginalized communities, a symbol of resilience and determination in the face of societal resistance.

Through her political journey, Charlotte continued to embody the power of love as a catalyst for change. Her unwavering commitment to inclusivity and equality transformed not only her own life but also the lives of countless others who dared to challenge societal norms and embrace love in all its beautiful forms.

As she fought for legislative reform, navigated the intricate world of politics, and advocated for the rights of all, Charlotte remained grounded in her core values, guided by the belief that love knows no boundaries and that equality should be a cornerstone of society.

Charlotte's journey served as a reminder that change begins with a single voice, with the courage to challenge the norm and advocate for a more inclusive and compassionate world. She stood as a testament to the power of love to drive societal transformation, offering hope and inspiration to those who longed for a world free from judgment and discrimination.

In the halls of power, Charlotte worked tirelessly to build bridges, shatter barriers, and create a more equitable future. Her journey was a testament to the unwavering spirit of love and the belief that, united, we can shape a world that embraces diversity, celebrates love in all its forms, and cherishes the fundamental principles of equality and acceptance.

Chapter 15 Redefining Love: Charlotte's Speech in the House of Representatives

In the grand halls of the House of Representatives, Charlotte stood at the podium, ready to deliver a speech that would challenge the traditional notions of love, family, and marriage. The room was filled with a mix of curiosity, scepticism, and anticipation. The weight of her words hung in the air as she began to address her fellow representatives.

"Ladies and gentlemen of the House, esteemed colleagues, I stand before you today to advocate for a new vision of love and commitment—one that recognizes the validity of a marriage between three individuals. The time has come for us to acknowledge that love is not confined by rigid structures or limited to the boundaries of societal expectations. Love, in its infinite and beautiful complexity, knows no bounds."

Charlotte's voice rang with conviction, her words resonating throughout the chamber. She painted a vivid picture of a world that celebrated diversity, embraced non-traditional relationships, and offered equal rights and protections for all.

"For far too long, our laws have failed to keep pace with the evolving dynamics of human relationships. We live in an era where love can no longer be confined to the traditional binary concept of marriage. Love is fluid, it is multi-faceted, and it can thrive within the context of a committed partnership involving three individuals."

She skilfully wove personal anecdotes, highlighting stories of individuals she had met along her journey, and their deep desire to express their love and commitment in a way that honoured their unique relationship structures.

"Behind every law, every policy decision, and every social construct, there are real people whose lives are impacted. We cannot turn a blind eye to the struggles faced by those whose love defies conventional norms. It is our duty as lawmakers to ensure that our legislation reflects the diverse reality of the world, we live in."

Charlotte continued to passionately articulate the need for legal recognition and protections for those in polyamorous relationships. She stressed the importance of fostering an inclusive society that embraces and supports all forms of consensual adult partnerships.

"Our Constitution enshrines the principles of equality and liberty, and it is our responsibility to uphold these ideals. Denying individuals, the right to marry based on the number of partners they love not only violates their fundamental rights but perpetuates discrimination and reinforces an unjust status quo."

She addressed the concerns of those who may question the practicality or feasibility of recognizing marriages involving three individuals. Charlotte presented comprehensive research, highlighting studies that demonstrated the stability, well-being, and success of polyamorous relationships.

"The research is clear: polyamorous relationships can be just as loving, committed, and fulfilling as their monogamous counterparts. By recognizing and legitimizing these relationships, we not only promote personal autonomy and freedom but also foster healthier and more honest connections."

Charlotte's speech resonated with some representatives who had previously held reservations, sparked thoughtful discussions and prompted introspection. She urged her colleagues to set aside preconceived notions and biases, to approach the issue with an open mind and heart.

"We must embrace progress and choose compassion over judgment. We have the power to redefine what love and family mean in our society. Let us stand on the right side of history, on the side of love, acceptance, and equal rights."

As her speech came to a close, Charlotte's words echoed throughout the chamber, leaving a lingering impact on the hearts and minds of those present. She implored her fellow representatives to consider the inherent value of love, and the profound impact that legal recognition could have on countless lives.

"Our duty as lawmakers is to protect and uplift the rights of all individuals, regardless of their relationship structures. We have the opportunity to lead the way in creating a society that embraces love in all its forms—a society that celebrates the diversity of human connections."

The applause that followed Charlotte's speech was a testament to the power of her words, the resonance of her message, and the impact she had made on her fellow representatives. While the journey to change hearts and minds was far from over, Charlotte's impassioned plea for love and equality had left an indelible mark on the floor of the House of Representatives.

As she stepped away from the podium, Charlotte knew that the road ahead would be challenging. But she was fuelled by the belief that love had the power to reshape the world. With unwavering determination and an unwavering commitment to her cause, she continued to fight for a future where love, in all its beautiful manifestations, would be celebrated, honoured, and protected by the laws of the land.

Charlotte stood before the conservative deputy; their ideological differences palpable in the air. It was the last session before the vote on the proposed law recognizing marriages involving three individuals. The debate had been fierce, emotions running high on both sides.

Conservative Deputy: Charlotte, I appreciate your passion, but I must express my concern about the impact of legalizing polyamorous marriages. Marriage has traditionally been defined as a union between two individuals, and altering this definition undermines the sanctity and stability of the institution.

Charlotte: I understand your concerns, and I respect your perspective. However, it is important to recognize that societal norms and understandings of marriage have evolved throughout history. We have witnessed changes that have expanded the definition of marriage to include individuals of different races, religions, and sexual orientations. It is only natural to extend that inclusivity to those in polyamorous relationships.

Conservative Deputy: But Charlotte, marriage is the foundation of our society. It is an institution meant to provide stability and support for raising children. How can we ensure that the children in these polyamorous relationships will have the same level of stability and emotional well-being?

Charlotte: I appreciate your emphasis on stability and the well-being of children. Research has shown that children raised in polyamorous families can thrive when they are surrounded by a loving and supportive environment. It is not the structure of the family that determines a child's well-being, but rather the quality of the relationships within it. By granting legal recognition and protections to these families, we can provide the stability and support needed for healthy child development.

Conservative Deputy: I fear that legalizing polyamorous marriages will open the floodgates for further redefinition of the institution. What's to stop people from demanding recognition of other unconventional relationships, like polygamy or even incestuous unions?

Charlotte: I understand your concerns about a slippery slope, but it is essential to distinguish between consensual adult relationships and those that involve coercion or harm. The law I propose is specifically focused on recognizing and protecting the rights of individuals in consensual and loving polyamorous relationships. It is about extending equal rights and opportunities to those who have been marginalized and denied recognition for far too long. We must approach this issue with nuance and ensure that we strike the right balance between personal freedoms and societal norms.

Conservative Deputy: I appreciate your perspective, Charlotte, but I firmly believe that traditional marriage should be preserved. Our society has functioned based on this definition for centuries, and altering it could have unintended consequences.

Charlotte: Change can be uncomfortable, and it is natural to feel a sense of unease when questioning established norms. But as lawmakers, it is our duty to adapt to the changing needs and realities of our society. Our responsibility is to protect the rights and well-being of all individuals, regardless of their relationship structures. By recognizing and legalizing polyamorous marriages, we can foster a more inclusive society that values love, commitment, and personal autonomy.

The conversation between Charlotte and the conservative deputy epitomized the clash of values and perspectives on the issue of polyamorous marriages. Despite their differences, both individuals held strong convictions rooted in their respective beliefs and understanding of societal norms.

As the session drew to a close, the time for the final vote approached. Each representative would cast their decision, reflecting their stance on the recognition of polyamorous marriages. The outcome would be a reflection of the collective will of the House, capturing the complex tapestry of beliefs and ideals that made up the diverse legislative body.

Charlotte remained hopeful that her impassioned arguments and the support garnered from her fellow representatives would pave the way for progress and equality. Regardless of the outcome, her journey had been one of resilience, courage, and an unwavering belief in the power of love to shape society for the better.

With bated breath, Charlotte awaited the results of the final vote. The tension in the air was palpable as each representative cast their decision on the recognition of polyamorous marriages. The room fell silent as the count began, and the anticipation reached its peak.

As the vote count progressed, it became apparent that the outcome was hanging by a thread. Every vote carried immense weight, and the future of polyamorous marriages rested on this pivotal moment. Charlotte's heart raced, her emotions running high as the tally continued.

Then, a wave of joy and disbelief washed over her as the results were announced. By the slimmest of margins, with just one vote beyond the majority, the legislation recognizing polyamorous marriages had passed. Charlotte's vision of love, equality, and acceptance had triumphed.

Tears streamed down Charlotte's face, a cascade of overwhelming emotions. Happiness, relief, and a deep sense of fulfilment welled up within her. She had fought tirelessly for this moment, pouring her heart and soul into advocating for the rights of individuals in polyamorous relationships.

The significance of the victory was not lost on Charlotte. It represented a profound shift in societal norms, a milestone in the recognition and acceptance of diverse forms of love. It was a resounding affirmation that love knows no bounds, that the bonds of commitment and dedication can transcend traditional expectations.

Amidst the jubilation, Charlotte found solace in the knowledge that her efforts had made a difference. She had given a voice to those who had long been marginalized, fighting for their right to love and marry in accordance with their authentic selves. The weight of responsibility settled upon her shoulders, as she understood that the real work had only just begun.

As the news spread, celebrations erupted throughout the polyamorous community and beyond. Messages of gratitude and admiration flooded Charlotte's social media platforms, reminding her of the impact her advocacy had made on countless lives. The outpouring of support from individuals who had yearned for recognition and acceptance was overwhelming.

In the midst of the jubilant atmosphere, Charlotte took a moment to reflect on her journey. She had faced numerous obstacles, endured scrutiny and opposition, but she had never wavered in her commitment to creating a more inclusive and equitable society. The road had been arduous, but the destination was worth every step.

With the passage of the legislation, Charlotte's dream of becoming a wife, of legally solidifying the bond she shared with Amelia and Mark, was finally within reach. The realization brought a renewed sense of purpose, of the profound love and dedication that had brought them together.

As she wiped away her tears of joy, Charlotte stood tall, ready to embrace the next chapter of her life. She would continue to fight for the rights and recognition of all forms of love, knowing that the struggle for acceptance was ongoing. Her victory was not just for herself but for all those who believed in the power of love to defy societal norms and transform lives.

With the knowledge that her advocacy had made a lasting impact, Charlotte pledged to use her position as a representative to champion further progress and equality. She knew that her role extended beyond her personal aspirations, encompassing the well-being and happiness of all individuals who yearned for love and acceptance.

In that moment of triumph, Charlotte took a deep breath, ready to embark on the journey of building a future where love knew no boundaries and where every person, regardless of their relationship structure, could experience the joy of being recognized, respected, and celebrated.

As she stood amidst the cheers and applause, Charlotte's heart swelled with gratitude, knowing that her determination and unwavering belief in love had brought about a profound change. With newfound strength and purpose, she would continue to pave the way for a more inclusive and compassionate world, where love would forever shine brightly, defying the constraints of convention and embracing the limitless possibilities of the human heart.

Chapter 16 The marriage of Charlotte

T hree months later, on a picturesque June day, the beach of Hampton transformed into a scene of love and celebration as Charlotte, Mark, and Amelia prepared to exchange their vows. The sun shone brightly in the clear sky, casting a warm golden glow on the sand and the sparkling ocean beyond.

As the gentle sea breeze caressed their faces, the setting seemed to reflect the serenity and joy that filled the hearts of the three partners. A beautifully adorned arch stood at the water's edge, adorned with flowers in vibrant hues of blush pink, soft lavender, and pure white.

The intimate gathering of guests, carefully chosen for their close connections with Charlotte, Mark, and Amelia, added to the sense of love and support. Ten cherished individuals, comprising friends and family, eagerly awaited the union of this unique trio.

Among the guests were accomplished singers and actors, friends who had touched the lives of Charlotte, Mark, and Amelia in profound ways. Their presence brought an added sense of enchantment and creativity to the occasion, as their voices and performances would weave through the ceremony, infusing it with an extra layer of magic.

As the time drew near, the beach became alive with excitement. A sense of anticipation filled the air, mingling with the gentle whispers of the waves and the soft murmur of conversations among the guests.

Charlotte's father, who had initially struggled to comprehend his daughter's unconventional path, stood at the altar, emotions tugging at his heart. He had witnessed Charlotte's journey of self-discovery, watched her fight for her beliefs, and finally, come into her own as an advocate for love and acceptance.

As he looked upon his daughter, resplendent in her bridal attire, a mix of emotions washed over him. Pride swelled within his chest, intermingled with a hint of nostalgia for the little girl he had once known. He was grateful that he had found the strength to embrace the uniqueness of her love and support her in this profound moment.

As the ceremony began, the sound of waves crashing against the shore provided a natural symphony, setting the rhythm for the exchange of vows. Words of love, commitment, and unity were spoken with unwavering conviction, punctuated by heartfelt promises to nurture and cherish their relationship.

The presence of a thousand attendees, including members of the community and advocates of love's boundless nature, lent an air of grandeur and significance to the occasion. The vast gathering stood as a testament to the power of love, transcending societal norms and embracing the possibility of deep and meaningful connections.

As the sun started its descent on the horizon, casting hues of orange and pink across the sky, the celebration continued with laughter, music, and heartfelt toasts. The atmosphere was electric with joy and love, as guests mingled, celebrated, and danced on the sandy shores.

In the midst of the festivities, Charlotte's father, a blend of emotions etched on his face, approached his daughter with a mixture of pride and tender affection. He took her hand in his, his voice slightly choked with emotion as he whispered, "Charlotte, my dear, I may not have fully understood your path at first, but seeing the love and happiness that radiates from you, I know that you have found your own unique journey. Today, as I stand here witnessing this beautiful union, I am filled with a profound sense of joy and gratitude. You have taught me the power of love and acceptance, and I am honoured to be your father."

Tears welled in both their eyes as they shared a poignant moment of connection, the bond between them strengthened by the journey they had embarked on together. In that instant, Charlotte's heart swelled with gratitude, knowing that her father had embraced the truth and beauty of her love.

As the evening progressed, surrounded by the love and support of their community, Charlotte, Mark, and Amelia revealed in the celebration of their unique union. Laughter and joy echoed along the shoreline, as the night became a tapestry of shared memories, dancing beneath the stars, and heartfelt moments of connection.

Their wedding on the beach of Hampton was not just a celebration of their love, but also a testament to the resilience of the human spirit and the transformative power of love that defies convention. It marked a significant milestone on their shared journey, as they forged a path that celebrated the beauty of their polyamorous relationship and paved the way for others to embrace love in all its boundless forms.

As the wedding festivities drew to a close, the guests raised their glasses filled with effervescent champagne, clinking them together in a resounding toast. Cheers filled the air, a collective celebration of the love and union between Charlotte, Mark, and Amelia.

With smiles of joy and gratitude, the newly married trio bid farewell to their loved ones, their hearts brimming with excitement for the adventure that awaited them. They stepped into a sleek, black limousine, the embodiment of elegance and luxury, ready to embark on their honeymoon in the enchanting city-state of Monaco.

Inside the limousine, Charlotte, Mark, and Amelia settled into the plush seats, their hands intertwined, their eyes gleaming with anticipation. The soft glow of the interior lights added to the romantic ambiance, casting a warm and intimate atmosphere around them.

As the limousine glided through the streets, the cityscape passing by in a blur of lights and colours, the trio shared tender glances and whispered words of love and excitement. Their hearts beat in harmony, as they revealed in the culmination of their journey and the beginning of a new chapter in their lives.

The anticipation grew as the limousine made its way to the airport, where a private jet awaited them. The thrill of embarking on this honeymoon adventure, hand in hand, was palpable. The thought of exploring the enchanting sights of Monaco together, basking in the beauty of the Mediterranean coastline, and immersing themselves in the rich culture and luxury of the principality filled their hearts with joy.

As the jet soared through the sky, carrying them towards their destination, Charlotte, Mark, and Amelia gazed out of the window, marvelling at the breath-taking views below. The moonlight danced on the waves of the azure sea, casting a shimmering path towards their honeymoon paradise.

In Monaco, their days were filled with enchantment and romance. They strolled along the pristine beaches, hand in hand, feeling the warmth of the sun on their skin and the gentle breeze rustling through their hair. They explored the opulent casinos and exquisite restaurants, indulging in delectable cuisine and savouring every moment of their shared adventure.

Each evening, as the sun dipped below the horizon, they would retreat to their luxurious suite, where panoramic views of the Mediterranean awaited them. The nights were filled with whispered words of love, passionate embraces, and the exploration of their deepening connection. In the embrace of their love, they discovered new depths of intimacy and shared moments that would forever be etched in their hearts.

Their honeymoon in Monaco was not just a lavish getaway but a celebration of their unique love and the unity they had forged. It was a time to nurture their bond, to revel in the joy of being newlyweds, and to reflect on the incredible journey that had brought them to this moment.

As their honeymoon came to an end, they returned home, their hearts filled with cherished memories and a strengthened love. Their marriage marked a triumph of love over societal norms, a testament to the power of acceptance and authenticity.

Together, Charlotte, Mark, and Amelia embarked on a lifetime of love, partnership, and shared dreams. Their union, forged in the depths of their hearts, was a testament to the resilience and beauty of unconventional love. With each passing day, they continued to challenge the boundaries of traditional relationships, paving the way for a world that embraced love in all its beautiful and diverse forms.

Conclusion

I n the closing chapters of this book, we witness the transformative journey of Charlotte, Mark, and Amelia as they navigate the complexities of love, relationships, and societal expectations. What began as a story of personal exploration and self-discovery evolves into a powerful narrative of acceptance, resilience, and the pursuit of happiness.

Through the pages of this book, we have witnessed Charlotte's unwavering determination to live authentically, to embrace her desires, and to challenge the limitations imposed by societal norms. In her quest for love and fulfillment, she finds solace and companionship in the arms of Mark and Amelia, forging a bond that defies convention.

Their path is not without obstacles. They encounter societal resistance, face judgment, and grapple with their own fears and doubts. However, their unwavering belief in the power of love propels them forward, guiding them through the stormy seas of opposition and leading them towards a brighter, more inclusive future.

As the narrative unfolds, we witness the growth and transformation of each character. Amelia, scarred by past experiences, learns to trust again and finds solace in the arms of Charlotte and Mark. Mark, initially hesitant but open-minded, discovers the depth of his capacity for love and the joy of embracing a non-traditional relationship.

Together, they navigate the complexities of their polyamorous journey, building a life and a family based on love, trust, and communication. With the birth of their children, Rose and Nate, they experience the joys and challenges of parenthood, further strengthening their bond and commitment to each other.

Throughout their journey, Charlotte emerges as a fierce advocate for love in all its forms. She uses her platform to challenge societal norms, penning a best-selling book and even entering the political arena to champion the rights of those in non-traditional relationships.

Her voice becomes a catalyst for change, inspiring others to embrace their own unique paths and challenging the boundaries of love and acceptance.

In the final chapters, we witness the triumph of their love as they celebrate their marriage, surrounded by loved ones and supported by a community that has embraced their unconventional union. Their journey is a testament to the power of love to defy societal expectations and the transformative impact of living authentically.

This book, a tapestry woven with love, passion, and resilience, seeks to expand our understanding of relationships, to challenge our preconceived notions, and to inspire us to embrace the boundless possibilities of love. It reminds us that love knows no boundaries and that, in a world filled with diversity, the pursuit of happiness is as unique as each individual's heart.

As we bid farewell to Charlotte, Mark, and Amelia, we are left with a profound sense of hope and possibility. Their story serves as a reminder that, regardless of the obstacles we may face, love has the power to prevail, to transform, and to shape the world into a more inclusive and compassionate place.

May their journey serve as a beacon of inspiration, guiding us towards a future where love is celebrated in all its magnificent forms, and where the bonds of connection and understanding transcend societal norms. And may we, as readers, be encouraged to embrace our own unique paths and to navigate the complexities of love with courage, authenticity, and an unwavering belief in the transformative power of the human heart.

Don't miss out!

Visit the website below and you can sign up to receive emails whenever Charlotte Rivers publishes a new book. There's no charge and no obligation.

https://books2read.com/r/B-A-MHOZ-CVVLC

BOOKS 2 READ

Connecting independent readers to independent writers.